PLEASE SAY YES

"Justice first," Lizzie said, when the crowd in her basement had quieted down. "How many of you feel that girls at Riverport High could use a little *respect*?" Fifty hands shot up. "And how many of you know that when we asked the boys to consider having our practice floor fixed so we don't have to slip and hurt ourselves during practice, we were insulted and told to *forget* it?" No hands this time, just an angry buzz.

Lizzie waited until the room fell silent. Then she said, "No guy holds your hand or kisses you or puts his arm around you until we get that floor *and* that respect. No boyfriend, no date, no guy you meet at Archie's or the movies or anywhere, anytime. Not until the boys' basketball team votes to give us what we need."

"Justice first!" Cara shouted. All of the team and some others shouted along.

I *hated* the plan because it meant I couldn't see Jeff for a long time. But I did want it to succeed. Lizzie looked at me, and tears streamed down my face. I nodded in agreement.

Bantam Sweet Dreams Romances
Ask your bookseller for the books you have missed

Please Say Yes

Alice Owen Crawford

BANTAM BOOKS
TORONTO · NEW YORK · LONDON · SYDNEY

RL 5, IL age 11 and up

PLEASE SAY YES
A Bantam Book / April 1984

Cover photo by Pat Hill

ISBN 0-553-24096-X

Published simultaneously in the United States and Canada

*Bantam Books are published by Bantam Books, Inc. Its trademark,
consisting of the words "Bantam Books" and the portrayal of a
rooster, is Registered in U.S. Patent and Trademark Office and in
other countries. Marca Registrada. Bantam Books, Inc., 666 Fifth
Avenue, New York, New York 10103.*

PRINTED IN THE UNITED STATES OF AMERICA

O   0 9 8 7 6 5 4 3 2 1

Please Say Yes

Chapter One

I was waiting for my brother after a tough basketball practice one cold November day, when I heard a soft voice behind me. "Marlene? You dropped something."

I couldn't believe my ears. Then I realized it had to be Dunk imitating Jeff Simmons's gentle southern accent to have a little fun with me. My brother can imitate anyone. And of course he knew perfectly well how much I liked Jeff—the name did creep into my dinner conversation just about every night of the week.

The very thought of Dunk playing such a filthy trick made me furious. I'm not like some younger sisters who worship the ground their brothers walk on. Dunk's just a big headache as far as I'm concerned. I was sure this was just another one of his annoying jokes.

So when I whirled around and found myself looking up into Jeff's sensitive green eyes, I was absolutely amazed. He was really shy with girls, so I'd never expected him to come right up and talk to me, as much as I'd dreamed of it.

I suddenly forgot about the chilly wind whipping through my thin corduroy jacket. Somewhere in the back of my mind, I was even grateful to Dunk for taking so long after his own basketball practice while I waited for him in the cold parking lot.

Jeff was wearing his dark green jacket—the one I like because it makes his green eyes seem three shades lighter. His curly black hair caught the orange glow of the November sunset, and his shy grin showed his perfect white teeth. What a beautiful face, I thought, looking at his high cheekbones. And let me tell you, the rest of him's not bad, either.

"Hi, Jeff," I said, trying to sound nonchalant. Jeff smiled shyly and held something out to me. It was one of my brochures for Rocky Mountain Adventure Tours. The trips were expensive, but I'd just about decided to take one in July. "Thanks," I said as he handed it back to me.

"You dropped it inside by the gym."

"That was nice of you to bring it all the way

out here." I couldn't believe he'd actually followed me and started a conversation. For a few moments, neither of us said anything. Then at last he spoke again.

"Are you going on one of those trips?"

"I think so," I said. "I've saved some of the money, and my parents said they'll make up the difference, so I'll probably go. I'm just trying to decide on the right one, although I've got a lot of time yet."

"They all look pretty good. Got it narrowed down any?"

"This one," I said, pointing to the panel describing three weeks to Pike's Peak. "I think I like it the best."

"The girl on the front cover looks like you."

"You really think so?" I asked, and he nodded. I mean, she was a *model*. She had long, dark hair cut pretty much like mine. And her face was the same type as mine, wide-set blue eyes, small nose, broad smile. And she was slim like me, with long legs and slender arms. With a little imagination, I could see me standing up there on Pike's Peak, waving at the camera just the way she was. But this girl was truly beautiful, and I'd never thought of myself that way.

I didn't know what to say, so I asked, "Do you have any plans for the summer?" What a stupid question, I thought. Just because I liked to plan ahead didn't mean that everyone knew in November what they were going to be doing in June. But Jeff didn't act as if he thought it was a dumb question.

"I'll be staying in town, that's for sure."

"Are you going to work?"

"Oh, yeah, definitely."

Neither of us could think of anything to say after that, so we just stood there and smiled at each other. Still, I didn't feel uncomfortable with the silence. After all, Jeff was finally making an effort to get to know me. It was too good to be true. Being on the basketball team, he probably had gotten the word from my loud-mouth brother that I really liked him.

Actually, I'd had the feeling for a while that Jeff was interested in me but that he was too shy to make a move. Why did I think that? You know how sometimes you'll catch a guy looking at you from the corner of his eye? And when you turn around he's suddenly doing something super-important like studying a picture of the 1970 football team? Well, that was Jeff.

"Where will you be working?" I asked finally.

"For my dad. He's a contractor. You know, construction. Usually, we work on private

4

houses, but there's the possibility of something really big this summer."

I was about to ask Jeff about the big something when a hideous noise shattered the romantic peace of the parking lot. "Wheeeeee-ooooooweeeee!"

If you knew my brother Dunk, I wouldn't have to explain where it came from. That was his own personal "Kung Fu Victory Cry"—not that Dunk knows anything at *all* about Kung Fu.

He covered the forty yards between the side exit and the place where Jeff and I stood in a few bounds. He hadn't bothered to dry his long hair after showering, so it flopped into his eyes with every leap.

"Listen to this!" he shouted right into my ear. "Some old geezer died last week and left five thousand bucks to the school."

"Jubilation," I said. "A new chem lab for us to toil and suffer in."

"Oh, no," Dunk crowed. "The guy's will says he spent the best moments of his life playing basketball for Riverport High."

"Thrill upon thrill," I said.

"Listen, twerp," he hissed, "the money goes to the school's athletic program." I perked up at that. I'm one of Riverport High's most enthusiastic female basketball players. "And that's not the best part," Dunk said, grinning. "The will says *we* get to decide how the money will be spent. It's all for the members of the varsity basketball team."

"Wow!" I exclaimed.

"Sounds great," Jeff said.

"Well, give some serious thought to how we should spend the money, Jeff old boy. You younger guys are going to be using the new stuff in the years to come."

Another of Dunk's delightful brotherly habits is trying to make himself sound mature and wise. He's only a year and a half older than Jeff and I are, and he sure isn't wiser! A quick glance told me Jeff didn't seem to be thinking about money at all. Instead, he was looking straight at me with an expression that's hard to describe, except to say that it made me feel very warm and sort of fizzy inside.

"Now, who wants a ride home?" asked Dunk, opening the driver's door of his old red Camaro.

Jeff and I got in, and Dunk turned the ignition key, but nothing happened. He tried again and again. Nothing, not even a half-hearted cough.

"Want to check it out?" Jeff suggested.

"Right," Dunk replied. "Let's check the

carburetor." I happen to know that Dunk wouldn't know a carburetor from a tailpipe. Which probably explains why Bucky Brown of Lucky Bucky's Auto Exchange managed to sell him that junkpile in the first place.

I wasn't looking forward to standing around in the wind again, but I figured I could help Jeff at least as much as Dunk could, so I got out and watched. Probably, Dunk had done something super-stupid like forgotten to buy gas. I sure hoped it was only that. The Red Wreck had made life much easier for me. Getting driven straight home after practice was great. And lots of times I could talk Dunk into giving me rides when I was going somewhere. It would be a real pain if something were really wrong.

Jeff started looking pretty worried as his hands moved across the engine, tugging here, pushing there. Dunk stared vaguely over his shoulder, muttering through clenched teeth.

"Amazing," Jeff said, stepping back from the car.

"Yeah? What?" Dunk asked nervously.

"Looks like the motor seized up."

"Oh, yeah," Dunk said. "I thought that might be it."

"Very rare. One chance in a thousand. I've never seen it before. The engine runs out of oil, locks, and nothing can move."

"Right." Dunk nodded.

It was interesting to watch Jeff take charge like that. No matter how obnoxious my brother is, I can see why most of the kids are a little awed by him. He's six-foot-three, wildly handsome, except for that stringy long hair, and the best basketball player at Riverport High. He'd kill anyone who called him Douglas, his real name. Anyway, the kids at school, including Jeff, usually let Dunk take charge.

But now the situation was reversed. Not that Jeff threw his superior knowledge about the car around. In fact, he did just the opposite. He didn't make a big deal about it the way Dunk would have.

Dunk bit his lower lip and said, "Let's say it *is* seized up, like we think. How much do they get for fixing a seized-up motor nowadays?"

"Can't fix it," Jeff said evenly.

"What?" Even in the darkening shadows, I could see the color drain from Dunk's handsome face.

"Motor's gone," Jeff said. "You'll have to put a new one in. Cost you a thousand, more or less."

Have you ever heard a Kung Fu death wail? Neither had I until Dunk made one up on the spot.

Dunk and I had just less than a mile to walk. Jeff came with us halfway, but real conversation was impossible with Dunk complaining the way he did. What was he going to do on dates, beg Dad to use the station wagon? Never! But would Kathy or Moira or Janie stand for taking the bus? No chance.

You get the self-pity picture. I had problems of my own. Mostly, I had to figure out how I'd get home from practice. Buses only ran every hour or so after five. And walking a mile every night as the weather got colder and colder just wasn't my idea of a good time. But I forgot all about that when all of a sudden Jeff took my hand, oh-so-gently, in his. At first, he was really casual about it. When I looked up at him, he was staring straight ahead. Then I squeezed his hand, just a little. I felt a slight squeeze in return. The corners of his mouth moved closer to a smile, but his eyes kept looking straight ahead.

OK, I told myself. You know he's shy. He's already started a conversation with you *and* taken your hand. What more do you want? Meanwhile, the warmth of his hand in mine made me forget about the cold. And when we got to where Jeff headed north, he gave my hand another squeeze and this time smiled down at me.

"See you tomorrow, Marley," he said very softly, looking right into my eyes.

"Sure," I said quietly. I could feel my heart beating very quickly.

Jeff's smile flashed again, and as he turned to jog up East Canal Drive, he gave me a wink.

"Late practice today?" Dad asked as we sat down at the dinner table later that evening.

"Don't tell me the coach made you run around the gym fifty times after practice again," Mom said, handing Dunk a bowl of steamed broccoli.

"No," he snapped. His rude tone killed the usually jolly mood at dinner before I could even get one bite.

"No?" Dad said patiently.

"No *what*, dear?" Mom added, even more patiently.

They'd both caught a hint of disaster, which is just what Dunk is when he's in a bad mood.

"No, we didn't have a late practice," Dunk growled.

"Why so late then?" Dad asked and smiled.

"I left my car at school."

"Oh? Why is that?" Mom asked, trying to sound cheerful.

"The engine seized up," Dunk admitted guiltily.

"I see," Dad muttered.

"Jeff Simmons looked at it. He said it's a real freak thing."

"Did Jeff Simmons mention a lack of oil as the cause of the motor seizing up?"

"I guess so."

"Would it be fair to say you forgot to put oil in?" Poor Dunk nodded. Instead of saying "I told you so," Dad said, "I'm sorry, Dunk." Then he reached out to give Dunk a friendly punch on the shoulder.

Dunk sighed with relief. He'd had a big fight with Dad three months earlier, when he decided to buy the car. He'd been saving his money for years, but Dad said he'd do a lot better if he waited until he graduated. Then he could get a really good car, something he could take to college, because he'd make a lot of money as a lifeguard over the summer. When Dunk insisted he needed the car before that, Dad had made another suggestion. He said he'd lend him the money in June, against his lifeguard salary. That way he'd have the car all summer. But Dunk still said he needed a car right away, so he went ahead and bought the crummy, broken-down old Camaro from Lucky Bucky.

"You learned a valuable lesson," Dad said,

taking a bite of his pot roast. "And you learned it fairly cheaply. If you'd ruined a *good* car this way, you'd feel an awful lot worse."

Dunk nodded some more. "I can get it fixed for about a thousand bucks," he said tentatively.

"You have a thousand bucks?" Dad asked.

"Not exactly."

"Can you get it?"

"Possibly."

"From where?"

"Um . . ."

"Yes?"

"How about if you lend it to me against my lifeguard wages?"

"Sorry," Dad said.

"Well, I've got some other ideas," Dunk replied.

I suddenly understood. Dunk was going to hit me up for my hard-earned, long-saved money, the money I was going to use to go to Pike's Peak that summer, all because he was too lazy to put some oil in his car. Well, I wasn't going to give it to him. But that didn't mean he wouldn't make my life miserable over it.

"Best of luck," Dad said sincerely.

"Best of luck," I repeated, not quite so sincerely.

Chapter Two

Rumors about the basketball money flew around school the next morning like the swirling flakes of a monster blizzard, and every rumor named a different amount. They reported anywhere from five hundred to five million! My extremely gorgeous friend Cara—big green eyes and a body that just doesn't happen outside of Hollywood—told me she heard the old guy left us $11,532.89. Because her figure was so exact, I believed her most of the day, until Lizzie gave us the true version.

Lizzie's the captain of the girls' basketball team. Her bouncy blond curls and baby blue eyes make her look kind of shy and naive, but she's nothing like that. She always stands up for what she wants. And she usually gets it. Not that I'm especially weak-kneed. But Lizzie never seems to lose her style.

Lizzie's a perfectionist, especially on the basketball court. Which, you can imagine, is tough if you're on the team. Every practice is as important to her as a game. Not that she yells at us for making mistakes or goofing off. All she has to do is give one look. But when she gives you that look of hers, you know it's time to shape up.

She's going out with Wally Peters, the manager of the boys' basketball team. He's also my brother's best friend. Wally's pretty obnoxious to me, but he really adores Lizzie.

Anyway, that day when the whole school found out about the old guy and his will and the money, Lizzie called a meeting before basketball practice. As soon as we'd all hit the locker room, she rapped the wooden bench with a shoe.

"I want to talk about this money," she announced. In three seconds flat we'd all moved close. "Since everyone in school's heard at least a hundred stories, I'm going to tell you the facts."

Lizzie looks especially pretty when she gets excited. Her eyes sparkle. "The news broke yesterday morning at a meeting of the athletic department, the principal, the dean and the old guy's lawyer. The guy willed five thousand dollars specifically for basketball, and the varsity players have a month to decide how it should be spent. They can do anything they want, as long as it's for the good of basketball at Riverport High."

"Can we bribe Skyhook Brooks to transfer here from Bay Channel?" someone joked.

When the laughter died down, Lizzie continued. "Right after the lawyer made his announcement, Coach Radburn suggested that *all* varsity basketball players should have a voice in the decision, including us."

Coach Radburn always looked out for us. It's a good thing she did, because girls' sports at Riverport High would have been a complete mess without her. The rest of the faculty didn't care at all about the program. The boys got first choice of everything—equipment, gym use—everything. They even got all kinds of publicity in the school paper, which we never did. I guess that's why so few of us girls thought we might actually get a share of the old guy's money. Even *we* had begun to think of ourselves as second best. Even with our winning record.

"Anyway," Lizzie said, "we all know how rotten our practice floor is, and I think it's about time we asked for a new one!"

"All right!" Cara called.

She's really outgoing, and she can steal the conversation as fast as she does the basketball.

"Be sure to read the *Riverport Report* tomorrow," Lizzie added. "It's got a terrific guest editorial that says *both* varsity basketball teams should decide how the money is spent."

"Don't tell me it was Freddy Barber's idea," Cara said.

Freddy's the editor-in-chief of the *Riverport Report*, and he's the *last* person you'd expect to take up the cause of equal rights. He once wrote a column saying the girls' team shouldn't get the same kind of varsity letters as the boys' team. He suggested ours should be pink.

"I said it's a *guest* editorial," Lizzie said and smiled. "And I'm the guest. Coach Radburn and I had a long talk about this situation after practice yesterday. We worked out some ideas for the editorial. The coach thought it would be a good idea to run it this week, so she talked to Ms. Bullfinch, and the Finch talked to Freddy."

The *Report*'s staff nicknamed their faculty adviser the Finch because her English accent makes her sound a little like a bird. She's really fantastic, and the kind of teacher who really cares about her students. All her students. You can go to her with almost any problem, and she'll be understanding.

After the meeting was over, we all cheered for Lizzie, Coach Radburn, and the Finch, finished dressing, and made lots of noise on our way over to the annex gym. We practice over there on the messed-up old floor. It's slippery in some places, sticky in others, and just generally full of splinters. Of course, we play games in the beautiful new gym where the boys get to practice all the time. Not too fair.

Still, we were all so psyched up about the possibility of sharing the five thousand dollars that we had one of our best practices ever. We were all playing like pros, until Julia Harrow, our five-foot, ten-inch center, slid on a slippery spot midcourt and twisted her ankle. Poor Julia didn't say a thing, but you could tell her foot hurt a lot. That's just like her. She's really sweet, so she didn't want to worry anyone, but there's no way she can hide her feelings. They show on her face.

Coach Radburn massaged the leg with ice for a few minutes and said Julia would be all right in a day or two. But we felt determined to get the new floor after that. It was a matter of safety.

The boys' team was still in the main gym

when we left. They were running fifty laps around the court as punishment for not working hard enough. They have to run laps a lot. The girls' team has a different system. We hustle. So, the boys usually get out a lot later than we do.

But that day Jeff had gotten out of his laps somehow, because he was standing near the exit door as I turned the hall corner. When I saw him, my heart started pounding, and I stopped dead in my tracks.

"You think he's waiting for me?" I asked Cara. I hadn't gotten to see him all day and had been really disappointed to see that the boys would be late. I figured there'd be no chance of bumping into him.

"Probably," Cara replied evenly. She knew all about my crush on Jeff, even that he'd held my hand the night before.

"Do you want me to leave?" she asked.

"Don't leave," I said. "I need some friendly support."

"Hi," Jeff said, looking up. He had the same green jacket on. I knew that lightweight wasn't warm enough for the blustery weather outside, and I felt a little shiver for him.

"Oh, no!" Cara cried, rolling her eyes dramatically.

"What's wrong?" I asked.

"I left my notebook in my locker. You go on, Marley. I'll see you tomorrow."

"OK," I said. What else could I say?

"Walking home?" Jeff asked.

"Sure."

He coughed. His face looked kind of flushed.

"Are you all right?" I asked.

"Not exactly. Coach Cassidy felt my head and sent me off the court. He said I must have a temperature of a hundred and two."

"I don't think you should walk home. One of the coaches can give you a lift. I mean, they can't refuse if you're sick."

"I didn't see you all day," he mumbled in his now raspy southern accent. There was a slightly embarrassed pause. "Think any more about your summer trip?" he asked softly as he held the front doors open for me. "Brr, it's cold out here."

"I'll probably do the Pike's Peak tour. Why?"

"Just curious." He turned his head to inspect something in the distance. I wondered if he was going to take my hand.

"Lizzie wrote an editorial for tomorrow's *Riverport Report*."

"About what?" he said.

I didn't want to distract him from remembering that my hand was dangling in the cold, practically freezing off. But I also wanted to know how he felt about the money and all. I took a deep, cold breath. "She thinks that *both* varsity squads should decide how to spend the guy's money."

"I don't know about that," Jeff replied. "You don't play nearly as many games as we do, right?"

"Yeah."

"And from what I hear the whole school turns out for our games, but—"

"That's right. We don't get half as many people for our games. But so what? We both play other schools. And we both get varsity letters. We work just as hard as you do, and we win most of our games, too. Besides, how are we supposed to get kids to come to our games when Freddy won't even mention us in the *Report*? How are we supposed to get better playing on that crummy practice floor? It's even dangerous! Julia slipped and twisted her ankle today. And this isn't the first time something like that's happened." All at once I stopped. I didn't want to antagonize Jeff—it's just that it was really important to me.

But instead of blasting me with a whole bunch of quick criticism, he thought about what I'd said for a few moments. Jeff was really something special. I imagined all the stupid things my brother, or Fred Barber, or lots of other guys would have to say. Not that Jeff would agree with me. But he'd taken a minute to consider my point of view. Finally, he turned and looked directly at me, eyes runny with cold and fever.

"Well?" I said.

"It makes sense."

"Really?"

"I never thought about it that way before, but what you say makes a lot of sense."

I couldn't believe it! I looked up at Jeff, and he smiled shyly. Not only was he the cutest guy I'd ever laid eyes on, but he was sensitive and fair, too.

"Listen," he said.

I did, but all I heard were our footsteps.

Then at last he said, "I was going to ask you out this weekend."

"Yeah?"

"I was going to ask if you wanted to do something."

"Like what?"

"A movie, maybe. But I don't know now. I've got a feeling my folks will want me in bed for a while."

"Oh, yeah." I felt like a Ping-Pong ball getting whacked back and forth between joy and disappointment.

"I may not be able to get out. But if I can, do you want to go out with me?"

Joy won the game with a powerful slam. "Sure," I said, deciding not to press my luck and slipping my ice-cold hand into my pocket.

Chapter Three

"What's for dinner?" I asked Mom that evening as I set the table.

"Tacos," she told me. "A new place opened up across the street from the library." That's where she works. "Torres Take-out Tacos."

"Olé!" I cried, clicking my fingers.

"There's no reason for me to be in the kitchen every night."

"I guess not," I said. I finished putting out the silverware and wandered upstairs to Dunk's room. I wanted to ask him what he thought about splitting the five thousand bucks with the girls' team. I didn't bother to knock, so I found him lying on his extra-long bed resting up from his fifty laps and gazing unhappily at the poster of the rock star Gloria Glory that he'd taped to the ceiling.

As soon as he saw me, though, his big green eyes grew bright and excited.

Some people are tricky. You never know what they want from you until they get it. Dunk, on the other hand, lets you know right off that he wants something, which puts you a step ahead of him.

I knew what he wanted. My tour money. "Forget it," I said.

"Forget what?" he asked innocently.

"Whatever. It's time for dinner." I was halfway down the stairs before his feet hit the floor, and I was sitting at the dinner table with my parents before he got a chance to bring up the subject.

My dad is very proud of the fact that he's got his own little business. He left a big accounting firm about two years ago and went out on his own. Now he's got three people on his staff, two younger accountants and a secretary. When something exciting happens down at Bennet Accounting, Dad likes nothing better than sharing it.

"We got our first audit," he announced, peeling the foil from his taco.

"From the state highway commission?" Mom asked.

I had this whole vision of the audit having to do with crooks who build roads and with bribery and that sort of thing. As I learned later, an audit is when you look through the record books to make sure money has been spent honestly and wisely. Dad had put in two whole days in Columbus, at the capitol, telling all the senators what a great accountant he was and how they should hire him to do their audits. He wasn't sure he'd get one, though, because his company was new and small. Now he was really psyched.

"We're on our way," he said and laughed. "Senator Fleming says he wants an honest, thorough audit, and that's just what he'll get. If anyone's been cheating the state, I'll dig out the information to prove it. Want to hear the plan of action?" he asked, then took a bite of the taco.

"Sure," I said. How boring could it be? But instead of continuing, Dad looked at Mom. I could understand why. The tacos tasted awful.

"I feel like celebrating my audit," he said. "What do you say I take us out to Lum-Lum's Szechuan Palace?"

"Perfect idea," said Mom, "we've certainly seen the last of take-out tacos!"

My friend Cara has this sixth sense about guys. She not only knows who likes her, but who *would* like her if she gave him a chance. If she feels like flirting, she knows where the guy will be when she wants to find him. More important, she knows which guys are sincere, which ones talk too much, and which are going to turn out to be babies.

The moment I heard the phone I thought maybe Cara's sixth sense had rubbed off on me. Why else would I have dashed into the house like a lunatic? Especially when nobody else even *heard* the phone ring? And I was weighed down by about four pounds of Lum-Lum dumplings, crispy chicken, and sesame noodles. Just walking was painful. But I went charging into the living room in spite of that because I somehow knew it was Jeff. The moment I heard him on the line, I could tell that our long stroll home hadn't done him any good. His voice sounded terrible.

"How'ya doing?" he said when I picked up the phone.

"Lost your voice?"

"You could say that."

"Does it hurt?"

"Not really. I just called to say I have to stay in bed. I've already been to the doctor."

"What's wrong?"

"Flu. So I called to say the date's off. I can't

go out for the rest of the week. I'm sorry, Marley."

"Your voice sounds like it hurts."

"Just a little."

I noticed my family tiptoeing through the living room. They were trying to look like they weren't listening, but my parents, like Dunk, are pretty bad at being devious.

"You think you'll be better Monday?" I whispered. I really didn't want my whole family listening in on my conversation with Jeff.

"What?"

"Will you be in school on Monday?"

"I can't hear you," he croaked. "Is *your* voice all right?"

I didn't feel like yelling into the phone that I had to whisper to get some privacy in my own house, so I put my hand over the receiver and said, "Do you mind?" They got the message and drifted away.

"I asked if you're going to be in school Monday," I said into the receiver.

"I hope so," Jeff said.

"Maybe we can do something next weekend," I suggested.

"No, we can't. I'm going to North Carolina to visit my mother's folks. We're spending Thanksgiving there."

"Oh."

"Well, I hope I see you Monday." He coughed again. It sounded awful. I heard a voice in the background. "I have to get off now," he said. "I'm giving the phone an infection."

"Wait," I said. "I can get your assignments and call you tomorrow. Should I do that?"

"Sure." He ran through the names of his teachers. "Gruber, Mills, Murphy, and Platt."

"Got it. I'll call you tomorrow."

"I'm glad *your* life is still in one piece," Dunk snorted as I hung up. He'd been sitting on the staircase, just out of sight. "I've got a question for you," he said.

I stepped over his lanky body on my way upstairs. "I've got an answer for you," I said, turning to look down at him from the top of the stairs.

"Yeah?" He looked up at me hopefully.

"Whatever your question is, forget it."

"Marley, my little yummy-bug, may I come in and shower you with kisses?"

My first reaction was to ask myself how Jeff Simmons managed to get into my house and up the stairs at nine-thirty at night, talking like Bugs Bunny playing a trick on Elmer Fudd. But I came to my senses in about four seconds, when Dunk entered my room. I threw my history book at him, and I'm a pretty good shot, so he had to duck fast.

"Peace," he said in his own voice as he handed me my book. "I've got an idea you'll really like."

"Fat chance," I replied.

"I'm thinking of setting up a double date for Saturday night. Me and Moira, you and Jeff."

I looked at him carefully. "Even if Jeff can't get his brother's car?" I asked. "Albert probably needs it Saturday night."

"Makes no difference at all," he answered. "I just want to boost your first big romance. I know old Jeff needs a little pushing, and I just want to help you, Marley."

"I'm really touched," I said coldly. "*Almost* as touched as I'd be if you got a college scholarship and left tomorrow." That was my first remark *ever* about his failure to get any basketball scholarships so far. It was a sore point with him. I guess I was madder than I thought about his imitation of Jeff. "Besides," I said, "he's got the flu, and he can't come out all weekend."

"Too bad," Dunk said, ignoring my nasty remark. "I was looking forward to it."

"Since when?"

"Since after dinner when I got the idea

from listening to you on the phone. But, uh, there *is* something else I'd like to talk over with you."

The money again. I knew I had to kill Dunk's plan right then, or I'd never have a moment's peace.

I stared at the center of his forehead as though I saw a big hole there. That's a trick Lizzie once showed me. It really gets a person's attention.

Dunk said, "What's wrong?"

"Have I got your attention?"

"Yeah." He looked unsure of what was happening.

"Good. I'm going to tell you something very important, so I want you to listen closely. You will not get your hands on a penny of the money I've saved up. It will not be poured down the drain on your car. I would rather walk ten miles in freezing weather every day of the week than give you my money."

"How about a loan?"

"No. It stays in the bank until I spend it. In fact, I will even break my rule about running to Dad and Mom if you pester me about my money."

"Aw, come on . . ."

"If you even *mention* the subject again, I'll

swear to them both you're making my life miserable with your constant nagging."

"But I'm desperate."

"And I'm very sorry."

And I must admit, as Dunk dragged himself out of my room, I really did feel sorry for him.

Chapter Four

Friday morning went very slowly. With Jeff home in bed, the *Riverport Report* was all I had to think about. To be honest, the *Report* did not have many readers that year. That was because the humor column wasn't funny, the news wasn't news to anyone, and the editorials sounded like Freddy Barber was standing in front of his mirror watching himself say big words. Exactly the kind of thing you try to avoid.

It was embarrassing, the way stacks of *Riverport Report*s just sat on the table in the main front hall at the end of school on Fridays. You'd think Ms. Bullfinch would have figured *some* way to make the paper more interesting. She certainly had the year before. Not that it was all her fault. Freddy Barber had a lot to do with it. I guess she thought it was a temporary lost cause and tried thinking ahead as much as possible.

That day, however, things were different. In fact, "different" doesn't begin to describe it. Copies of the *Report* were almost all gone when I got to the front hall before lunch. There weren't even any crumpled up on the floor. Instead, I saw people actually engrossed in reading them. I grabbed one from the dwindling pile and turned to the editorial page. There was Lizzie's Guest Editorial asking for a voice in deciding how to use the basketball money and explaining all about the lousy, dangerous practice floor. But right next to it was a really *digusting* editorial by editor-in-chief, Freddy the Fool. This is what it said:

DRAGGING THE VARSITY DOWN

Men's basketball is the most important sport at Riverport High, a sacred tradition etched in the legend of our glorious school throughout its long history. Our famous rivalry with Bay Channel High is known throughout the state as an example of red-blooded competition unparalleled in the annals of amateur sport. Walking among us, the varsity basketball *man* strides confidently and with the attitude of a warrior prince carrying the imperturbable honor of a reverent constituency on his strong shoulders. Let us not denigrate this heroic figure and all he represents! Let us always honor these brave athletes.

The *girls'* basketball team is something else. It is, in this observer's honest opinion, not really a sport at all but just a way for the little ladies to keep fit. They play only a few games all season. To laugh? No, no. That would be ungentlemanly. But should we consider this a *varsity* team in the full sense of the word? Should we disparage the memory of our gallant late alumnus and make a mockery of his generous gift by forcing our courageous basketball team to give up its role of honor? Certainly not! For when all is said and done, the girls' so-called "basketball team" represents virtually nothing. The men were given the money, not the girls. Let's keep it that way!

Half the kids in the main front hall were pasting their eyeballs to copies of the *Report*. The other half were watching those who were reading to see how they reacted to the two columns.

Most of the guys smiled. A few laughed out loud. I *did* hear a couple of guys criticizing Freddy Barber, thank goodness. *None* of the girls were smiling. I saw a lot of angry faces, and there was some pretty bad language thrown around.

Then I saw Julia, our center on the team, the one who got hurt because of the bad practice floor. She was standing in the corner near the big trophy case, tears trickling down her cheeks. No one's ever accused Julia of blinding speed either on her feet or between the ears. But no one's ever accused her of an evil thought, either. She may not be the brightest girl at Riverport High, but she's one of the nicest. I walked over to where she stood.

"Do you worry what that moron Freddy thinks?" I asked her.

"I guess I do," she said and sniffled.

"Oh." What else could I say? "How's your ankle?"

"I'm OK. I was lucky." Julia wiped her tears away as she walked down the hall.

I will not even try to describe my feelings at the moment because if I did, all you would read would be a long, ugly string of words. But I'll tell you what I did. I headed for the basement office of the *Riverport Report* to find Freddy. As small groups of girls moved with me through the hall leading to D-wing staircase, I realized I was not alone. About twenty-five of us gathered outside the *Report* office, sounding like a swarm of angry bees discussing targets for mass attack. And the sight of Lizzie, hands on hips in front of the door, convinced me that blood would flow. She tried the door and said, "It's locked."

"I bet the ghoul went home," someone shouted.

"Where does he live?" someone else called out.

"What seems to be the problem?" Ms. Bullfinch's bell-like voice pealed as she walked calmly into the crowd. She stopped when she got to Lizzie. What a sight! The two of them facing off, nose to nose!

Then, after a few seconds, Ms. Bullfinch smiled. "We're on the same side, you know." She sounded as grand as Queen Elizabeth.

"Why'd you let him do it?" Lizzie demanded.

The Finch looked around, then raised her voice so all of us could hear. "A lot of people share his point of view. The *Report* is supposed to express the different opinions of the students of this school. In addition, I stretched the rules a bit when I allowed your editorial to appear at short notice. The editor-in-chief wanted to reply, so I really could not deny him the space. When I saw what he'd written, I felt exactly as all of you do."

I looked around. A few boys had joined the growing crowd.

"However, as you know, this paper does not go in for a great deal of faculty censorship," she continued.

No one could deny that, not after last year's editor wrote about our crummy school lunches and about the junk food machines in the halls and about how local school board members went on vacation with people from the company that owns the machines. A lot of us were amazed that such things got in the *Riverport Report.* And a lot of us also thought somebody would get in trouble. Like the editor, or Ms. Bullfinch. Instead, the paper got a national award in a high-school newspaper competition, and the junk food machines got removed. So the Finch had a point about censorship.

"Besides, I think Freddy's piece may be quite good for our girls' athletic program." There were gasps all around.

"How?" Lizzie asked.

"No one can ignore the issue now. My advice is to keep your heads." The Finch's cultured English voice grew soft. "Let the thing settle. By early next week we'll have a good idea where matters stand."

Lizzie nodded. You could almost see the wheels turning in her brain. She wasn't one for sitting around and waiting for things to settle.

"And now," Ms. Bullfinch said, "I've got work to attend to. Just one more thing. Consider Freddy Barber under my personal protection."

Lizzie laughed. "All right."

The Finch's pale, delicate fist rapped lightly on the office door. "It's Ms. Bullfinch. You can open up now, Freddy."

As soon as I got home after practice, I called Jeff with his homework assignments. That was the second time I had called him that week. It was getting to be a habit—a nice one.

"You sound terrible," I said when he answered.

"It's not bad because I've got something nice to think about."

"Really? Oh." I realized he was talking about me, and I felt my own temperature jump a point. "Well I hope you feel better soon." Sounding like a get-well card was the best I could do after his dreamy, romantic words.

"What's happening about Dunk's car?"

"Nothing. He's really moping about it."

"Maybe he'd like to double sometime. I mean, I can use my brother Albert's car sometimes. Maybe Dunk would like to come along. With you and me, I mean."

"I bet he would."

"Not if you don't want him to."

A wave of guilt broke over me. After all, Dunk had been pretty generous with his car when it was still around. Now that it was broken, he didn't have any way to take his girlfriends out. Well, Janie had a car, but his really serious girlfriend, Kathy, didn't, which put a damper on their relationship. "Sure he can come. Help the hopeless, that's my motto."

Jeff's laugh sounded like one of those jackhammers they use to break up the street, except, of course, much weaker.

"Here are your assignments. Got a pencil?" I gave him the information. Then I said, "You want to hear something really disgusting?" He didn't say no, so I read the entire text of Freddy's editorial, "Dragging the Varsity Down." As you would expect, I got madder and madder as I read. By the time I finished, my temperature was probably higher than Jeff's. "How about *that* slime?" I snorted at the end.

"Sounds like something a fool would write."

Then I read him Lizzie's editorial about both teams working together to create a fair and sensible plan for spending the money. I figured he'd love it. "What do you think of *that*?" I asked.

"Hard to say."

"Oh, yeah?"

"Well, a lot depends on how the boys want to spend the money in the first place." A long, loud cough interrupted him.

"Don't speak another word," I said. "It hurts you too much."

"Then *you* talk awhile. I like to hear your voice."

"Oh. Sure. OK." Well, I admit there was a slightly long pause before I could think of what to say next. I didn't want to go on about the basketball question. What if we didn't agree? I didn't want him steaming away while I piled my viewpoint on him, or else jumping in to argue when every word hurt his throat. I didn't want to talk about anything boring. *What* could I talk about?

I quickly remembered Jeff's interest in my summer tour, so I sort of reviewed the different trips they offered. I'd been talking for five or six minutes when he interrupted.

"I've got to get off now," he grated. I had the funny feeling I'd picked the wrong subject.

"OK. Take care of yourself," I said. I wanted to say a lot more than that, but I didn't have the guts.

"Yeah. You, too. 'Bye."

After I hung up, I felt both excited and a little upset. I felt great about talking to Jeff, but I didn't like the way he had suddenly gotten off the phone.

I forgot about the conversation with Jeff, though, when Dunk showed up three minutes before dinner. He'd been hanging out at Archie's combination Poison Pizza and Addic-to-Vision. By which I mean to say that some people spend a lot of time in there with nothing to show for it but bellyaches and no quarters left in the world.

Dunk's attitude had undergone a change for the worse. Make that the worst. For openers, he met my cheery hello with stony silence. More chilling yet, he spoke to Mom and Dad in a quiet, extra-polite voice, as if someone had sewn up his windpipe so only this tight little sound could get through. Mainly, he used three sentences.

One: "Yes."

Two: "No."

Three: "I don't want to discuss it."

He kept that act up all through dinner, even when we discussed Freddy's insulting editorial. He didn't even try to avoid infuriating everyone. He insisted on saying "yes" and "no" in all the wrong places and "I don't want to discuss it" every time you asked him to explain a really absurd "yes" or "no." For example, Dad said, "You actually *agree* with what that gibbering nincompoop wrote about the girls' team?" and Dunk replied, "Yes."

"Surely you don't approve of his insulting tone?" Mom asked.

"Yes," Dunk said.

"Doesn't it bother you that *I'm* one of his victims?" I demanded.

"No."

"You still upset about the car?" Dad inquired.

"I don't want to discuss it."

"OK," I said, "I'm sorry for what I said about the scholarships."

"*What* did you say about scholarships?" Mom asked.

Then my dad the diplomat closed the whole subject by saying, "Can't we find anything else to talk about over dinner?" We couldn't.

Later on, I knocked before entering Dunk's room. He'd just finished getting dressed to go out and was wearing a dark blue shirt and jeans.

"Going out with Moira?" I asked.

"No."

"How come?"

"I don't want to discuss it." He gave a bit of a snarl there.

"Where are you going?"

"Kathy's."

"Going to watch TV and so forth?" He didn't answer. "Listen, Dunk," I said, "you don't really *agree* with Freddy Barber, do you?" He stared at me. "C'mon," I said.

He shrugged to show how little it mattered to him. "I don't want to hurt your feelings, so why don't we not discuss it?"

Remember when I saw Julia crying in the front main hall and I asked her if she cared what a moron like Freddy thought? And she said she guessed she did? Well, ten seconds later I was flat on my bed, crying into my pillow because another moron, Dunk the Dope, wouldn't stand up for the girls' basketball team!

After that, a chilly atmosphere settled over the house. Dunk and I hardly said a word to each other all weekend. By Sunday afternoon Mom and Dad were asking questions. Not that they got any answers. Dunk and I agreed on one thing, at least; it was a private feud.

Even Jeff's phone call failed to change things. He said Albert had offered him his car for getting to and from school until the doctor declared him completely well. Albert is twenty-two. He's an assistant store manager and has an apartment a couple of blocks from his family's house, but he said he would ride to work with his dad while Jeff used the car.

"I'll pick you up at eight tomorrow morning," Jeff said. "Tell Dunk he's got a ride, too."

I did, later that night, through clenched teeth.

"I've already got one. Janie's picking me up," he replied coldly. I started to retreat from his doorway when he looked up and growled, "You and your friends can just forget about that basketball money."

"Hey," I said, "just because *we* have personal problems—"

"Buzz off, twerp."

So I did.

"Dunk's not coming," I told Jeff as I got into his brother's silver Toyota.

He smiled. "Good. I just thought I should make the offer."

We cruised slowly down the block in silence. Then he blurted out, "I don't know if there's any reason to tell you this, but I have a girlfriend back home."

"Home?" For some weird reason I thought he meant his parents rented part of their house.

"In North Carolina. We've been writing since I left. And we talk on the phone sometimes."

"Oh." I guess something must've shown in my face because he started talking faster than I'd ever heard before.

"I mean I'm going to see her when I go back Wednesday. And I'm going to tell her that I don't feel the same way I did when I left."

"Oh? You sure about that?" I *sounded* calm, anyway.

"Maybe I shouldn't have told you about her," he said. Silence. He shrugged. We stopped for a light.

"Maybe you feel guilty about asking me out before you talked to her about it," I said. He nodded. "How long were you going out with her?"

"Two years."

Now I felt my bones melting inside me. They were practically married! How could a couple of walks home possibly make a dent in Jeff's two-year, soul-deep passion for this hometown girlfriend? He'd tell her, all right. He'd get about a sentence into his little speech and then forget the rest when she took his hand and hypnotized him with eyes as big and blue as the Atlantic Ocean. And once their lips met? Well, you could just forget his teensy little romance with Marlene Bennet!

"Want a ride home after practice?" He smiled as we walked across the parking lot.

Where was my pride? My integrity? My sense of honor and dignity? "Sure," I said.

Chapter Five

The next few days were awful. Dunk and I continued feuding. Lizzie and Wally were in the middle of their first fight, and boy, was it a big one! The rest of the girls on the team were pretty steamed up, too. And it wasn't just us. Many girls who'd never even dribbled a basketball were furious about the whole thing. The Finch was right when she said Freddy's article would make the issue a big deal. It *was* a big deal, now.

On Wednesday, the day before Thanksgiving break, Lizzie called a meeting of the girls' basketball team. As soon as the last bell rang, we hurried to the locker room and gathered eagerly around her.

"In ten minutes," she announced, "Marley and I are going up to the dean's office." That was certainly news to me, but I just shrugged my shoulders and listened. "We're meeting with representatives from the boys' team, the president of the student council, Freddy Barber, and assorted others. We're also going hear from the late Leo Appleton's lawyer about the money Mr. Appleton left us." Everyone began hooting and hollering at that, but Lizzie silenced us with a wave. "Don't cheer yet. I don't know what we'll find out. But I'll come straight to the gym when it's over."

"Why me?" I asked as we hit the hallway.

"You represent the non-starters and non-seniors. And if this meeting turns into a shouting match, you'll be a good person to help out."

The first person we saw when we walked into the dean's office was Lizzie's boyfriend, Wally. It was pretty weird the way they didn't even smile at each other. Needless to say, they were on opposite sides of the debate over the money. After all, most of Wally's friends were on the team, and if they were determined to keep the money for themselves, Wally would have a hard time going against them. Especially since he's the team manager and is supposed to represent the majority's opinion. On the other hand, he was crazy about Lizzie. They usually agreed on *everything.*

Wally spoke for the boys' team, along with Jim Trumbo, their muscular, super-macho captain. Geraldine Phelan, the president of the student council, glared angrily at Freddy Barber, who fidgeted nervously under her gaze. A few kids from the student council, the honor society and the varsity club were there, too.

A skinny, elderly man wearing a gray flannel suit sat patiently waiting for us to settle down. Lizzie and I took seats across from Wally and Jim, kind of like a showdown. After what seemed like a long time, the elderly man got up and began to speak.

"Young ladies and gentlemen, I am Mr. Dankers, the late Leo Appleton's lawyer. Mr. Carter has asked me to clarify the terms of my client's bequest, and I feel I must explain to you that Mr. Appleton's will refers to the members of *the* varsity team. At the time he made out this will, in 1956, there was only *one* varsity basketball team, and it was the *boys'* team. I'm afraid the will must be interpreted in this way. It refers to the boys' varsity team only. *This* team must decide how to spend the money. Thank you all for coming." That said, he got to his feet, slipped into a snappy tweed topcoat, wished us a pleasant afternoon, and left.

The grin on Freddy Barber's face almost bought him a one-way ticket to the underworld, but I was distracted quickly by Dean Carter's powerful voice. "I've a few more things to add. I called this meeting in order to hear your ideas and to get some basic facts across to the student body. There are a number of points to be considered."

Dean Carter really was a great choice to run this meeting. He's one of the most liked and respected people in the school administration. Of course, the kids in that room were not troublemakers, but even a few of *us* could remember moments when a less sensible, less kindhearted dean would've made life pretty difficult. At least, that's what I thought before he started to speak again.

"In the interest of fairness, the school board will make it known to the members of the boys' varsity that at least ten percent of the money must be set aside for new girls' uniforms."

"Five hundred dollars out of five thousand?" Lizzie said in a very low voice.

The dean looked slightly uncomfortable. "Of course, the boys may decide to share any amount with the girls' team, for any purpose that benefits basketball at Riverport. As long as ten percent is set aside for girls' uniforms."

"Who decided on uniforms?" asked Geraldine Phelan.

"The school board," Dean Carter answered.

"How come?" Lizzie asked.

Dean Carter answered, "I really don't know. But that's what they want."

"What we *really* need is to have our practice floor fixed."

"Yeah," I chimed in. "We could make our own new uniforms if we wanted."

"Now, now ladies, don't get carried away," Freddy said, smirking. He was hiding safely behind Wally and Jim.

"The problem is," Jim spoke up, "we want the bleachers and backboards painted, we want a new scoreboard, new uniforms, new basketballs, and some work on our own floor. And after we do all that, I don't believe there's going to be enough for work on your practice floor. Isn't that right, Wally?"

Poor Wally. He usually agreed with everything Lizzie said. Now he had to choose between the girl he adored and all his friends on the basketball team. He looked pretty terrified at the moment, and he didn't say a word.

"Listen," Lizzie said heatedly, "Julia Harrow got hurt on that floor last week. It wasn't serious. None of the many minor accidents have been. So far. Does one of us have to get really messed up before something's done about that floor?"

"Well, don't get so offended," Jim said sarcastically. Then his voice softened. "Lizzie, we're not saying you girls shouldn't have a better floor, but why should *we* buy it for you with *our* money?"

"Oh, come on, Jim. You know the school doesn't have extra money for the sports program right now. You do, and you want to use it for all sorts of stuff you don't really need. In the meantime, we're hurting ourselves."

"Well, that's just not our responsibility. The money is ours!"

"May I offer a suggestion?" Dean Carter said. "We've still got almost a month to work this out. I think the members of both teams should talk it over with their coaches and each other in order to find a solution everyone can accept. We have a wonderful opportunity here, and I'd hate to see it cause anger instead of happiness. But, girls, the decision belongs to the boys in the end, so you'll have to appeal to them. They may choose to give you the floor."

To which Jim Trumbo replied softly, "No chance."

"Fine," Lizzie replied angrily, "but if all we end up getting of that five thousand dollars is five hundred, let us spend it the way *we* choose, not on uniforms we don't need or want!" And with that, she stormed out of the room and back to the annex gym, dragging me along.

By that time practice was almost over. When we came into the gym, everyone looked at us, even though they were in the middle of a practice game. They were trying to figure out what had happened upstairs. I think it was pretty obvious from the disgusted expressions on our faces.

As soon as Coach Radburn saw us, she blew her whistle for time out. "OK, girls, let's have a full report." Amid groans from the team, Lizzie explained the whole awful story. When she was done, Coach Radburn said she thought we should talk to the boys immediately. She said she'd slip over to the main gym and ask Coach Cassidy for a little post-practice meeting. Meanwhile, we hit the locker room.

"What now?" Cara asked, pulling off her sweaty shirt.

"We make an appeal to their conscience," Lizzie answered.

"Right," I said. "Can we bring a microscope to find it?" Everyone giggled.

"We'll get our floor fixed." Lizzie's tone killed the giggles. "The first step is to state our case calmly and reasonably to the boys' team."

"And if it doesn't work?" Cara inquired.

"We'll cross that bridge when we come to it. Now I want volunteers."

"For what?" I asked.

"I need some moral support. So who's coming?"

She'd have gotten a better response selling antarctic snorkeling outfits to overweight ostriches.

"No guts?" said Lizzie, quite calmly. "I'll do all the talking. You won't have to say a word."

Cara sighed. "I'll go." She could afford to, I told myself. She could bat her eyes and stick out her magnificent hip at the first sign of trouble.

"Me, too," Julia said.

We all looked at each other in shock. I pictured her standing by the trophy case, tears rolling down her cheeks. Julia was so quiet, everyone's friend. No one expected her to get involved in this mess. The look in Lizzie's eye told me she was surprised, too.

"Well, I did just get hurt," Julia explained.

I was giving serious thought to the lifelong emotional damage this might cause tender-hearted Julia when I heard Lizzie say, "Good, that does it. Me, Cara, Julia, and Marley."

Everyone cheered. "Hey!" I said.

"Meeting adjourned," Lizzie shouted over the uproar, wrapping up the second volunteering session of my day.

Just outside the door of the main gym, Lizzie had us all join hands, like we did before a game. "None of you has to say a word," she whispered. "All we have to do is stay calm and look strong."

When we walked into the main gym, we found all sixteen members of the boys' team, including Jeff, assembled together in the bleachers. Jeff looked a little pale. The boys were wearing their usual attractive collection of old sweat suits, ripped shorts, headbands, etc. Wally and Jim, of course, were wearing their regular street clothes since they'd been up at the dean's office. They sat with Dunk in the middle of the crowd.

There were some barnyard sounds as we walked in, but Coach Cassidy ended them with one loud roar. Anyway, things had quieted down by the time the four of us stood there facing them; Lizzie a little in front, Cara and me to one side, Julia on the other.

"Well, you all know why we're here," Lizzie began. "It's simple. We need to have that floor fixed a lot more than you need anything done up here. It's a matter of safety. We think fixing our floor will do the most to help basketball at Riverport because it'll make the biggest improvement."

"The dead guy was talking about *real* basketball," someone said.

Lizzie ignored him. "We agree it would be nice to fix this place up." She looked around the gym. "We play five games a year on this court, so we know we'd benefit, too. But it's a luxury we can all easily do without. Getting our floor fixed is a necessity."

Then, to everyone's amazement, Julia stepped forward. "Lizzie's not kidding. I twisted my ankle because of a slippery spot last week." I'd never heard her so angry. "I don't want to go through pain like that again just because you boys are too selfish to do the right thing!"

I couldn't believe what happened next. Gordy Fellows, senior and starting forward, spoke half under his breath. He said, "Getting your nose fixed is the right thing."

To which Cara, in a moment of understandable outrage, shouted, "How 'bout a skin job,

Scabbo?" This was a nasty reference to Gordy's acne. I don't deny that Cara's remark was pretty mean, but what Gordy said back was so terrible that I can't repeat it here. Also, I can't quote what I said to Gordy, what Gordy said to me, or what Jeff said to Gordy. I can't even repeat what Coach Cassidy said as he jumped onto the bleachers to help Jim and a couple of sophomores pull Jeff and Gordy apart.

In fact, the next thing I can report is what Coach Cassidy shouted to us after he'd separated Jeff and Gordy. "That's enough. Go on now, girls."

I waited just long enough to make sure that Jeff wasn't hurt, at least not too badly. We were almost at the door when Jim's rough voice caught us from behind. "Hey, girls!" he yelled. We stopped and turned. "You had your say. Here's your answer. No."

Most of the boys cheered, and my own brother was one of them. Boy, was I furious with him! He hadn't said one word to defend me.

"So now what do we do?" Cara asked as we walked back to the locker room to get our things. "We'll talk about it tomorrow," Lizzie said. "Until then, no discussion at all." We shrugged, then nodded.

"Bunch of doofs," whispered Julia.

*　　*　　*

Despite Lizzie's not wanting to discuss it, Cara provided a highly thrilling instant replay for the rest of the team still back at the lockers. They'd hung around after practice to see what had happened.

Lizzie let her finish and then said, "Saturday afternoon there will be a meeting at my house. I want everyone here to show up." She looked around the room until everyone had nodded back to her. "I want you to do something else."

"What?" Cara asked supiciously.

"I'm going to name girls I want at the meeting. Each time I call out a name, I want someone to volunteer to make sure that that girl gets there. You don't have to come with them because I want you there early—two o'clock. I just want you to convince the other girls to show up. At exactly two-thirty."

"But what *for*?" Cara insisted.

"I'm keeping that a mystery. That way, you'll all be sure to come, just to see what's up. But you can tell your people we're going to make sure the boys do the right thing."

Everybody hooted and hollered enthusiastically over that. Except me. I was too anxious about getting outside to check up on poor Jeff and the wounds he'd gotten defending me. I wound up responsible for Melanie, from my math class. Then I got out of there fast.

Sure enough, there was Jeff waiting for me by the exit sign. "You OK?" I asked.

"Except for feeling like a fool." No blood. Not even any Band-Aids.

"Thanks for sticking up for me in there."

"Yup. One thing, though."

"Yeah?"

"Well, before this whole thing happened, I offered Dunk a ride." He could tell how thrilled I was at that because he added quickly, "Hey, I'm going to leave him off at Archie's."

It was certainly one of the strangest rides I've ever taken anywhere. I mean, the three of us had just been through this bizarre experience. I was furious at Dunk. Jeff wasn't, but he'd just gotten in a fight with a teammate who Dunk seemed to agree with. And Dunk couldn't even look me in the eye. No one said a word all the way to Archie's. Anyway, it was a major relief when my revolting brother got out. I gave him a really nasty look as he slammed the door of the Toyota.

"I think you girls should have a decent floor to practice on," Jeff said, turning to face me.

"I knew you would."

"But I also think we have to respect the old guy's will. He wanted to give something to his old team, the boys' team. He could have just given the money to the school, but he didn't. He wanted us to be able to use it as we wanted. But I'll tell you right now, I'll vote for as much money as it takes to fix your floor," he said.

"What if you're the only one?"

"Then we lose, I guess." He leaned over and turned off the ignition. It looked like this might be a long conversation.

"But you know that isn't right. The bleachers don't need to be painted, and your equipment is almost all new."

"But whatever we spend on the main gym benefits you, too, because you play home games there, the same as we do."

"Right," I agreed, "but none of those things is really *necessary*. Fixing our floor *is*, and we'll never get it done unless we use this money."

"That's true. I'll back you up the best I can."

"I don't think it'll be enough. Jim's really got an attitude. Most of the seniors will stick by him. And with the seniors against us, what kind of chance do we have?"

"Not much," he conceded.

"How many guys do you think will vote for us?" I asked.

"Not many. Me, two or three second-stringers and maybe another two or three who didn't let on."

"Dunk and Wally?"

"They didn't say much of anything."

"Not even to Gordy Fellows?" That really hurt. I mean, it felt wonderful to have Jeff defend my cause, but it was pretty painful that my own brother didn't.

"Marley, I know you're really upset about what happened in there. I am, too. But I don't want to talk about that now." He paused. "My flight leaves at nine tonight. I'll only be gone a few days, but I want you to know that I'm really going to miss you."

Then he looked straight into my eyes, and I knew what was going to happen next! He leaned down and pulled me gently to him. Then he kissed me, the softest, sweetest kiss in the whole world. I didn't want it to stop—ever. Afterward, we just sat there smiling at each other. Finally, he turned on the ignition and drove me home. He kissed me again before I got out of the car at my house.

Two more conversations rounded out my day, one disturbing, one delicious.

The first occurred as I was reading in the

little room off the kitchen. It's got a bed in it, which guests use, and I like to study in there. The phone rang, and Dunk picked it up in the kitchen. "Hey, Wally," he said. Somehow he failed to notice me lying there quietly with my book.

Sure, I could have made a noise, but I was too busy trying to get a sense of the conversation. Mostly, Dunk said, "no kidding," and "hey, man . . ." and so on, but after awhile, he began to talk more.

I figured out that Wally was calling because he and Lizzie had had a gigantic fight after the scene at school. I wasn't surprised. After all, Wally hadn't said any more during the fight than Dunk had, that is, not a word. He was definitely against sharing the money with us, which was a total insult to Lizzie and the rest of us. And Lizzie's not one to sit around quietly when she feels insulted.

What did amaze me was that Wally seemed to be asking Dunk's advice on how to patch things up. I couldn't understand why. If I wanted to know how to go about seeing three guys at one time without getting killed, I'd ask Dunk. But to help patch up a mature relationship built on respect and caring? It was like asking Ronald McDonald to recommend a vegetarian restaurant.

Here's what Dunk said: "You've got to make her feel like you need her. The trick is to *do* whatever you want but make her *think* you can't live without her." There was a pause, and Wally said something that, of course, I couldn't hear. Then Dunk said, "Believe me, it works every time." Another pause. "OK. Here's one I used on Kathy, Janie, and Moira last month. You say, 'Listen, I've been having these really gruesome nightmares lately. I usually wake up screaming—except after I've been with *you*. That's the only time I sleep in peace.' " Pause. "Sure, it worked great on all three girls." Then a really long pause. "OK, if you don't like that story, we'll think of another one. Right. I will. Don't worry. Talk to you soon."

Pretty repulsive, huh? Well, I was just lying there staring at my book, telling myself Dad and Mom had been the victims of hospital baby-switchers and Dunk wasn't really my brother, when the phone rang again. I felt that sixth sense come alive and jumped for it.

"Hi," said a wonderfully familiar voice. Just hearing Jeff cleared my head, and suddenly Dunk didn't matter in the least.

"Hi," I said, remembering our first kiss. "Where are you?"

"I'm at the airport. I just called to say good-bye again. Know what I'd like to do?" he said.

"What?"

"Repeal Thanksgiving."

Let me tell you. The shiver those words gave me lasted a good half a minute and passed through every inch of me.

"Me, too." That night, I went to sleep very happy, in spite of everything.

Chapter Six

As I walked into the basement of Lizzie's house Saturday afternoon, I was handed a round, gold pin. "What's this?" I asked.

"Just put it on." Lizzie smiled. I took a closer look. It was exactly like our blue and gold school pin but without the blue. I shrugged and clipped it to my shirt.

I glanced around the basement. About twenty girls were sitting around, all looking slightly confused. No one knew any more about what was going on than I did. The whole girls' basketball team was there. So were Geraldine Phelan, the student council president, Pixie Deverow, the head cheerleader, and Carol Stein, the honors club president. In fact, most of the popular, influential girls at school were there.

"Do you know what Lizzie's up to?" I whispered to Cara.

"Beats me," she said.

Then Lizzie started talking. "I got you here before the others because I want you all to be *ready* for what happens next," she said excitedly. "It's going to strike a lot of people as strange, but I think it can work *if* the idea is taken seriously this afternoon. I know we can count on every girl on the team. Geraldine, Pixie, and Caroline have already told me they're with us." She was certainly building suspense. "When I spring this idea on the rest of them, it's absolutely vital that everyone who's here now show enthusiastic support."

"What *is* it, for goodness' sake?" Cara asked.

"Just another minute," Lizzie replied. "There will be about twenty-five more girls showing up here soon. They're either cheerleaders, people who've been especially close to members of the boys' team, or else girls who a lot of people look up to for one reason or another. If we can win them over and get them to lead the school by example, we win. OK?"

My blood ran a little faster with anticipation. But when she finished telling us the plan a few minutes later, I wished I'd never heard of it or of Lizzie or even basketball for that matter.

"My gosh, are you *crying*?" Cara whispered amidst the cheering.

"Justice first," Lizzie said, about an hour later, when the whole crowd had been crammed into her basement and quieted down. It certainly got their full attention. She went on. "How many of you felt personally insulted by Freddy Barber's *disrespectful* article on girls' basketball?" Fifty hands shot up. "And how many of us believe that girls at Riverport High could use a little more *respect*?" Again the hands went up. "And how many of you know that when several of us went upstairs to ask the boys to consider having our practice floor fixed so we don't have to slip and hurt ourselves during practice, we were insulted and told to *forget* it?" No hands this time, just an angry buzz.

"I think it's time we taught the Freddy Barbers and Jim Trumbos and Gordy Fellowses at Riverport High a little bit of a lesson," Lizzie called. The crowd of girls responded with shouts of "Yeah!" and "Let's do it!" and "How?"

"Everyone got their buttons on?" Lizzie cried.

One big shout ripped through the crowd.

"Good, because they mean we *demand* a decent floor for the girls' practice court. And when we demand that, we demand respect for *every* female at Riverport. And when we get that new floor, we *get* that respect!"

Everyone cheered. I cheered, too, in spite of how miserable I felt at the moment.

"Justice first!" Lizzie shouted at the crowd.

"Justice first!" we all roared back.

Lizzie waited till the room fell silent. Then, in a low, hypnotic voice she said, "Your buttons mean that no guy holds your hand or kisses you or puts his arm around you until we get that floor *and* that respect. No boyfriend, no date, no guy you meet at Archie's or the movies or anywhere, anytime. Not until the basketball team votes to give us what we all need. Any questions?"

"Justice first!" Cara shouted. All of the team and some others shouted along.

Pixie Deverow said, "No cheerleaders at their games until we win. No girls at all at their games until we win!"

"Excuse me," Moira Rizzuti said. She's one of Dunk's girlfriends, also one of the most gorgeous and stylish girls at school.

"Yeah?" Lizzie asked.

"You really think this plan will work?"

"I'm positive."

"Well, I'm not so sure," Moira replied. "And *until* I'm sure-I don't think I can go along—"

But even before she'd finished her sentence, yours truly had streaked through the crowd and grabbed her arm. I had to stop her before she turned some of the girls against Lizzie. I *hated* the plan because it meant I couldn't see Jeff for a long time. But I wanted it to succeed more than anything.

"Shut up and listen to me," I whispered to Moira. Lizzie saw me and took all eyes away from us by saying our campaign would last about three and a half weeks because that's how long the boys' team had to make their decision.

"Dunk's never had a real nightmare in his whole life," I hissed. "He's too stupid even to think up a nightmare. He probably remembered it from a *Heavy Metal* comic book." The look in Moira's eyes told me I'd scored. I went in for the kill. "Ask Kathy and Janie about his little nightmares. They've heard the same story."

Of course, Moira dated other guys besides Dunk. Still, she didn't seem to like the idea of being fooled. My guess is, she'd believed the nightmare story. Anyway, she took a moment, then whispered back, "OK, I'm with you." She raised her hand and said, "You've got a point, Lizzie. Justice first."

"Margaret?" Lizzie looked at Gordy Fellows's girlfriend.

"Justice first!" she shouted.

Lizzie named a few more girls who hung around with basketball players, and they all yelled, "Justice first!" She didn't have the heart to call my name, though. My misery over not being able to see Jeff had now teamed up with shame and guilt over having just ratted on my own brother, even if he was quite a rat himself. My eyes were filled with tears. Lizzie just looked at me, and I nodded.

She went on to say that we should all wear our buttons and give more of them out to other girls. She talked about what we'd do if the administration tried to make rules against the buttons (which she didn't think they would) and other important topics. She went on to spell out a few more details. We could talk with guys as much as we liked as long as we made some reference to "the cause" in each conversation. Also, she said it might be nice to substitute "justice first," for "hello," "goodbye," and other greetings.

Julia asked why *all* the boys had to be undated and untouched. Lizzie said that hundreds of unhappy guys would put terrible pressure on the boys' team to vote right. And every girl in school had a stake in the outcome.

"Just one more thing," she said. "As we work for victory—and I know we'll win—don't let anger and hatred distort this noble cause. Remember, these are the same guys we'll be with again when the battle's over. As you struggle, look ahead. Let the boys know it's nothing personal. Make sure they understand that. Because when the victory is won, you'll be back with them again." Pretty inspiring, I have to admit.

As the crowd made its way upstairs, I stood in the corner of Lizzie's basement with Cara. "It's a good thing I've got strong nerves," I said, "or they'd be shot by now."

"It's only for a few weeks." Cara put her arm around me and grinned. "It's a great plan, Marley! And it's got to work."

"You know what I was thinking on the way over here?"

"What?" Cara's high spirits didn't help me any.

"I thought how I'd jump into Jeff's brother's car Monday morning and give him a really good welcome home."

"Relax," Cara said and smiled. "He's not sick anymore, so he won't have an excuse to drive his brother's car."

71

"I hope you're right," I said, still depressed.

"Justice first!" Cara shouted to the others as we left.

"Justice first!" they shouted back.

I wasn't looking forward to dinner Saturday night. For one thing, we were having leftovers, something Mom called "Turkey Surprise." Dunk's mood had only gotten worse since the blow-up in the gym. And considering the new developments in the girls' strategy, I really hoped there'd be something else to talk about over the meal.

There was, but it was still a completely depressing topic. Dad was upset about his audit. He stared at the tablecloth for a few minutes while everyone else ate quietly. Then he blurted out, "Some bozo called me from Senator Fleming's office yesterday." My dad sometimes thinks about things awhile before he says anything.

"Oh?" Mom looked wary.

"The senator's assistant. He told me to take it easy on the audit."

"What does *that* mean?" Mom asked.

"Just what it sounds like. They obviously don't *want* an honest audit. The guy named three companies in particular. I checked the assistant out. He's been with the senator for three years, so I have to assume he speaks for him."

"I'm so sorry," Mom said.

"One thing's for sure. If I ignore what he told me and get the wrong people mad, I'll never get another audit job from the legislature." Everyone was silent until Dad looked around and asked, "What do you think I should do?"

"Tell the guy to lose himself," I declared, using a forked stringbean for emphasis. "What do you want to be a crook for?"

Dad looked at me thoughtfully. Then he looked at Dunk. I didn't expect him to abandon his basic three sentences, but when he did, I couldn't believe my ears. "It depends what you want. If you want to be a big hero and show the world how honest you are, then you should tell the guy you don't want his business. Of course, that also means you'll just let some other guy get the job, and he'll probably be a *real* crook who doesn't even *try* to be honest. And of course doing that won't help anything except your own opinion of yourself. But if you want to make a better living and, you know, maybe get some more jobs with the legislature, then you should do what the guy says but stay as honest as you can. Know what I mean?"

"Yes," Dad said shortly, his lips pressed in a grim line. "I do." He took a long breath and turned to Mom.

She forced a smile and said, "You know what I think."

He nodded. "Of course." Then, without warning, Dad clapped his hands very loudly and said, "Well, enough of that!"

No one said much else for the rest of the meal.

Jeff called that night, long distance. "Having a good Thanksgiving vacation?" he asked.

"Not especially," I said.

"I had a long talk with Kim."

"Who?" Uh-oh. Kim from North Carolina.

"I told you I was going to talk to her."

"Don't tell me about it now. Tell me when you get home." I figured that if Kim had stolen Jeff's heart back, I'd rather spend Sunday oblivious before the tidal wave of disappointment flattened me.

On the other hand, if Jeff had dropped her, I really didn't want to give him the story on our romantic freeze campaign—"Lizzie's War," as people were calling it—over the phone. Especially not when he could rethink his decision about Kim. Either way, a face-to-face discussion on Monday morning seemed best, so that's what I suggested.

"Sure," he said. "Pick you up on foot at quarter to eight."

"OK."

"Bye." And just before he hung up, he shot me a long-distance kiss.

Chapter Seven

Sunday was the longest day of my life. I just couldn't stop thinking about Jeff. What would he say to me? And what would I say to him? By Monday morning I was so nervous I jumped about two feet when the doorbell rang.

"Who's that?" Dad called from the kitchen breakfast table.

"Jeff," I answered, opening the door.

My dad made a quick entrance, whipping off his glasses, and stuck his hand out. "Pleasure to meet you, Jeff," he said.

"Thank you, sir."

"You kids need a ride to school?"

"We're walking," I said.

"Thanks just the same," Jeff said and smiled, giving Dad's hand one last shake.

"Kim already had a boyfriend," Jeff said as we reached the sidewalk.

"Yeah?"

"Harley Roots." He smiled. "I went to first grade with him."

"Didn't she tell you about him before? In her letters or on the phone?"

"Nope," Jeff said, still smiling.

"Well, how'd you feel when—"

But Jeff cut me off by sweeping me into his arms and giving me the longest, sweetest kiss I'd ever dreamed of. Right there in the street! I guess I should have been embarrassed or worried about breaking Lizzie's rule about no kissing, but I was too overwhelmed by the ecstasy of it. After we started walking again, however, my eyes began to water up.

"What's wrong?" Jeff asked anxiously. I knew he was worried about having offended me. After all, people don't usually burst into tears when kissed.

I took a deep breath, then told him what had happened in Lizzie's basement and that I'd sworn off kissing. I told him that our little embrace just then was one of the best things I'd ever done but that it was also the last time I could do it until the boys on the team came to their senses.

My mom always said she never really knew

my dad until she had her first terrible argument with him. Her words came back to me now because that's just what I found myself in the middle of with Jeff. At first, he didn't say anything, just stared off into space. But he was giving off vibrations that brought the temperature down a few degrees. I could tell he was really angry.

"What's the matter?" I had to ask a few times before he decided to answer me.

"It's wrong, and it's stupid."

"No, the boys are wrong, and our plan will set them straight."

"How do you know?" he challenged me.

"Lizzie says it will." I knew that sounded pretty immature, but Jeff was nice enough not to ask if I'd run around waiting for the sky to fall just because Lizzie said so.

"I told you what I think," he said. "We boys have to decide this ourselves. That's what the old man wanted, what he meant when he wrote his will. He was thinking about a bunch of guys like him and his friends."

"But we need a new floor so badly! You know we do."

"And I'll try to get it for you. But not because of this—this—plan." He said the word as if it were the worst insult in the world. I was pretty stunned by Jeff's reaction. Kind, sensitive Jeff didn't understand any of our plan. Now it was my turn to give off icy vibes. Jeff nudged me gently. "Besides," he said, "there's no way this thing can work."

"Why not?"

Jeff shook his head. "Because you girls won't be able to stick together."

"Oh, no?" I said with determination.

"Of course not. You'll see. As soon as a guy gets fed up with being frozen out and tells the girl to forget it, another girl who liked him all along is just going to take her gold pin off and move right in."

"You think so, huh?" I tried to look as certain as I sounded. Jeff just nodded. "You think you know everything," I said nastily. "Don't flatter yourself!"

But secretly, I was scared he was right. After all, Lizzie's War had just started, and it was already causing problems between Jeff and me. And he was on our side!

He sighed. "It's a lousy idea. It goes against what the old guy wanted, and it'll just get the boys' team madder and meaner than ever. The girls won't keep to it, anyway."

"That's what *you* say."

"Yup."

"What about you and me?" I asked softly.

"What do you mean?"

I swallowed hard. "Are you going to get fed up by us not, y'know. . . ."

"Touching each other?" he said, raising his eyebrows.

"That's right. Are you going to tell me to forget it and wait for somebody else to move in?"

Some people pick the stupidest times to smile! Which is just what Jeff did. It was a cute smile, all right, but I sure didn't need him looking more wonderful than ever at that moment. "I'm not telling," he said, his eyes twinkling.

"What's that supposed to mean?" I demanded.

"You asked if I'm going to say 'forget it,' and I just told you I won't say anything."

"Oh."

He tried to get his smile under control, but he couldn't. It got bigger and bigger. "But I'm not worried," he said.

"You think I won't be able to hold out, either!"

Jeff was practically ear to ear smiles by now, and I was getting pretty fed up. "Look," he said more seriously, "let's not make this a personal fight, OK? I can go on as long as—"

"As long as I can stand not kissing you?" I snapped.

"For as long as I have to. I'm not interested in anyone else. I haven't been since I transferred here last year. I know it's not the best time for me to say it, but it's the truth." Well, how mad can you be when a guy says something like that? We walked on in silence, with me having some very serious thoughts about how long I'd really be able to keep from—you know. As a matter of fact, kissing Jeff was the only thing I could think about until he shook his head, turned to me, and said, "I'll tell you something else."

"What?"

"I'll do everything I can to *stop* Lizzie's War."

"How?" I asked. No answer. "I *know* you can't," I said, hoping to trick some kind of explanation out of him. It didn't work. He just shrugged. But at least he'd wiped the smile off his face.

We didn't say anything else all the way to school. And as we got closer to the building, I began to feel a little funny walking with him. After all, I should be setting a good example for the other girls. As we turned to go different ways in the front hall, I said, "Justice first," and waved.

That day the more I thought about the conversation with Jeff the angrier I got. Jeff was starting to seem even worse than Dunk, Jim,

Gordy, and the others. Because *they* didn't know any better.

But Jeff *did*, and that made it all the worse. He knew we needed the new floor, and he was taking a really snotty attitude about how we were trying to get it. He acted as if the dead guy's ghost were visiting him personally and telling him just what the will meant. Jeff made it seem as if he were the only one in the entire world who knew all the rights and wrongs of the situation. I can't *tell* you how mad I got every time I thought about his saying he was going to stop Lizzie's War. "Fat chance," I said under my breath.

If you already suspect that the entire week went from bizarre to bonkers, you have scored a bull's-eye. For example, the next day, Tuesday, Freddy Barber planted himself outside the lunchroom and handed out copies of something he'd written called "Proclamation." As you would expect, it was very difficult to understand. But the main idea was that the male half of the school had to support the boys' team. The crowd of girls that gathered around old Freddy was getting almost violent. And this time, neither Ms. Bullfinch nor a locked door could save him. Lizzie and I had to do that.

As we approached the lunchroom, Lizzie was just telling me about a problem with Cara. Then we noticed girls sort of shoving and bumping into Freddy. By the time we got there, his hand outs were on the floor, and his glasses were half off. Freddy Barber might be a toad, but he had guts. I had to give him credit. So did Lizzie. And between the two of us, we got the girls to spare his worthless life. Of course, Freddy went right on handing out flyers!

Anyway, the problem we had with Cara was this: Lizzie heard that she had made a date with a certain varsity basketball starter—and she'd promised to remove her gold pin for an hour. I hate to tell you who the guy was. It makes me a little sick to think of it. I just couldn't believe she'd go out with Jim Trumbo, team captain and main enemy of the cause.

Well, right before practice I dragged Cara down the hall and confronted her. "A girl on the team overheard your new sweetheart bragging to his friends on the bus," I said.

At first Cara denied it, but from the way she avoided my eyes, I knew the rumor was true. Finally, she shrugged and said, "Big deal."

"How come you want to hang out with *that* creep?" I asked.

Cara shook her head. "I don't know. It just came over me. All of a sudden he started to appeal to me."

"You've got to be strong," I told her. "You've got to stick with your friends on this. For all of us. For me."

Cara's large green eyes met mine for the first time. "What about you and Jeff? Don't tell me you're not having a hard time. The whole school knows the two of you are crazy for each other."

"So?" I said. She didn't know just how much I wanted to feel Jeff's arms around me, his lips touching mine.

"So don't tell me you two aren't cheating," Cara said.

"We aren't." I was really offended.

"C'mon, Marley. You can be honest with me."

"It's true. We aren't."

I watched as her face showed astonishment. Then when she realized I was telling the truth, she looked truly sorry. "I thought everyone was cheating," she replied at last. "Anyway, a lot of people."

"Not me." I shook my head. "Not Lizzie or Pixie or Geraldine or lots and lots of others."

"Oh."

"You've got to stick with us," I said.

"Oh."

I pressed on. "So can you, Cara?"

"Yeah. I can. And I will. You've got my word, Marley. I'll do it for you, and for the others. For *me*!"

Only about twenty girls, none of them cheerleaders, showed up for the boys' first game Wednesday afternoon, and every one of them left by halftime. A group of us waited outside the gym and gave each girl a gold pin as she left. And most put them right on. I know the absence of girls at the game had some effect because Riverport lost, 90–30.

Since boycotting the game didn't mean boycotting players *after* the game, I spent about half an hour cleaning out my locker until I heard the boys starting to come out of their locker room. Then I walked to the side exit and waited for Jeff.

When he came out, he was walking with Dunk, who kept going right past me without a word or a smile. Did I mention that Dunk's a sore loser and takes a day or so to recover from a bad game? Thank goodness Jeff stopped.

"I hope you're not here just to gloat," he said. Then, when he saw the slightly wounded look on my face, he said, "Sorry. I know that's not why you waited. I'm glad you're here."

"Good," I said, telling my hand to stay in my pocket and not grab his as we started the long walk home together.

"I played practically the whole game," he said.

"Great."

"Not really. Coach Cassidy only put me in because everyone else was playing so pathetically. I mean, Jim got nine points the whole game. And Gordy got only seven."

"What about Dunk?"

"Eleven or twelve, I think. But the twerp he was guarding scored more than twenty. He was six inches shorter than Dunk, and he must've taken about five hundred shots. Dunk did the worst of all."

"Oh."

"We had three cheerleaders, all of them guys. After a while they started making up phony cheers."

"Like what?"

" 'Riverport High, it's not time to die. Go team go.' " Jeff didn't seem to think that was funny, so I tried hard not to smile. "I hate to admit it," he said, "but it's starting to get to a lot of us."

"What is?"

"Lizzie's War." My heart jumped with excitement. Our first victory. Then Jeff added quickly, "It's only been a few days, Marley. But I'll admit the game was really painful. I mean, when you play for the school, you expect to have girls there. It's *part* of it. I saw the two worst high-school teams of my life this afternoon, Parsons and us. Except we're really a good team. We should've gotten a hundred points instead of thirty."

"Thirty? I didn't know it was that awful." I could see that our campaign was blasting team morale to bits. "I'm sorry," I said sincerely.

"Well, it's your responsibility, yours and the other ringleaders'. And the sad thing is, it won't help you get your floor fixed."

"It may."

He shook his head and tightened his lips. "First of all, it's just getting the guys more convinced that they're right. Second, Lizzie's War is almost over."

"Yeah? Where'd you hear *that*?" He wouldn't say another word on the subject. That got me more and more irritated as we walked on. "You're not as smart as you think you are," I said.

"You know why you're getting mad at me now?" he smiled, not so nicely.

"Why, Mr. Self-Appointed Genius?"

"*You* know," he teased.

"Oh, *that*," I hissed, trying to show how

deranged I thought he was. "You actually think I'm getting angry because I can't stand not kissing you."

Jeff grinned. "I didn't say that."

"But you're thinking it."

"How do you know what I'm thinking?" We walked the rest of the way to my house without talking. That was getting to be a new habit.

Then he said, "Now I'm thinking about kissing you goodbye."

Do you think he was purposely trying to drive me crazy? At the time, I did. "Don't strain your brain," I snapped, then turned and walked up the steps.

Chapter Eight

On Thursday we played our first game of the season. Guess who showed up to watch? I mean aside from Jeff; his brother Albert, who had Thursdays off; a lot of boys who came to boo us; and practically every girl in the school; plus most of the girls from Bay Channel High, who came to support Lizzie's War, even though they were our biggest rivals. Guess who else? A crew from the local "News at Six" TV program. They drove down from Columbus. Unfortunately, they got there an hour early so they could interview a whole bunch of people, and then they stayed for only a couple of minutes of the game. I didn't get to play until the second quarter, long after the cameras had left. And I didn't get interviewed because Jeff and I were having another little argument about you-know-what in the annex gym.

I didn't care, though, because I played almost half the game and scored fifteen points. Even Jeff forgot our spat after a couple of minutes and cheered so loudly I thought he was going to lose his voice again. And after the game, he was waiting for me. Of course, Albert was waiting with him. I suspected that Jeff had wanted Albert to come to the game to meet me. Why else would someone who's twenty-two come to a high school girls' basketball game on his day off?

But I didn't mind. It was sort of a relief. With someone else around, there was less chance of arguing. "Great game," Albert said after Jeff introduced us. He's a little shorter and heavier than Jeff, but almost as handsome.

"Thanks." I tried to look modest. I had to work on it because my basketball playing had never attracted much praise before. The fact is, we'd done to Saint Theresa High what Parsons had done to the boys' team the day before. I mean, we'd always been a good team with a winning record, but Saint Theresa's was one of the best teams in the state.

Anyway, I squeezed into the front of Albert's Toyota between the handsome Simmons boys.

I decided that wasn't really touching, so I wasn't breaking my promise to the girls.

When we pulled up in front of my house, Jeff said, "You going to catch the six o'clock news?"

"I guess so," I said. "You?"

"I guess so."

I nodded. "Well, so am I."

"Me, too."

We might have kept that up until the news was over, but Albert finally lost patience. "Both of you out!" he ordered in this real older-brother voice. "I'll pick you up at seven, Jeff. Unless that will interfere with your dinner?" he asked, looking at me.

"Oh, no," I said. "Mom had to work late. And Dad's taking her out to dinner, so we're just"—I saw a strange look in Jeff's eyes—"eating leftovers." Then I realized that Jeff's look was a challenge! His eyes said, "I bet you can't sit in that empty house with me until seven o'clock without any kissing or hugging."

"Well?" I tried to sound stern and impatient, like Albert. "Are you coming in, or what? We don't have much time."

"Yeah, sure," he said, getting out of the car. We waved goodbye to Albert and went into the house.

We took off our coats, and I hung them in

the hall closet. Jeff was wearing a tight green turtleneck. It really showed off his muscles, and it made his eyes seem greener than ever. But I didn't let it get to me. I forced myself not to look twice.

"Would you like to share some leftovers?" I asked and headed into the kitchen.

"Like what?" he asked, following me.

"Eggplant something. It has different things in it and tastes sort of like garlic."

"Eggplant something sounds great," he said and flashed this really charming smile.

It was almost six, so I just had time to dump the eggplant into a pan and put a low flame under it.

"Dunk home?" Jeff said.

"No. He probably went to Wally's for dinner. He usually does when nothing's cooking here."

"Looks to me like something's cooking." I wouldn't exactly use the word "fresh" to describe Jeff's tone of voice. But then again, he wasn't looking at the eggplant when he said it. Where was the shy boy who could once hardly talk to me?

"Well, nothing is," I informed him, "except for dinner. Can I get you something to drink?"

"Oh, no," he replied. "I'll just wait for the eggplant. We going to watch the news here in the kitchen?"

"If you want," I said.

"No, I'd rather watch in the living room."

"How come?" I asked suspiciously.

"Bigger set." He smiled.

"Oh, all right," I said, again trying to imitate Albert's impatient voice. We went into the living room, and I switched on the TV.

"You're really very good," he said, taking the middle of the sofa so that if I sat on it I'd have to be right next to him. I sat down on one of the arms.

"Good at what?" I said. "Heating up eggplant?" I really hoped he wouldn't say something stupid, like "Heating up me." That's what Dunk would say under similar circumstances.

"Basketball," he said. A toothpaste commercial came on.

"Oh. Thanks."

"I really studied you every minute you were on the court."

"Oh? Are you going to give me basketball tips?"

"If you like," he said. "After this is over and we can make a little contact." He smiled. "Your defense is a little weak."

"Maybe," I said. Speaking of defense, his incredibly handsome face was weakening mine again, so I jumped up and said, "I've got to stir the eggplant. Call me if we're on TV."

I'd been stirring for about five minutes when Jeff yelled, "Hurry up, Marley. It's us. Riverport!"

I turned off the flame and rushed into the living room. In fact, I rushed so fast that I accidentally sat right next to Jeff on the sofa. Not touching him, of course, but close. Too close. And I couldn't hop over to the other end. That would have been really obvious. So I just sat there and concentrated very hard on the screen.

Our spot lasted only about three minutes, but just about everyone was on it. First, the announcer said the real story was not the game, but the big "Riverport War" over the athletic budget. If you want to know the truth, she got the whole thing about as wrong as she could.

"I thought they always got everything right on the news," I said.

"Me, too," Jeff agreed.

Now, strange as it seems, these two little words made a big impression on me. Why? Because Dunk, Wally, Jim, and every other guy I knew would have said something like "How could you be so dumb?" or "Everyone knows they make mistakes," something to make themselves look cool. Not Jeff. Innocent as his remark might have been, it made me want to kiss him even more.

I kept my eyes on the TV for most of the time that Lizzie's face was on the screen. And while I don't remember much of what she said, I do recall thinking that she sounded great, really intelligent and certain of herself. Next came Freddy Barber and Jim Trumbo. Jim did a good job of saying "um" and "like, y'know" a lot. Freddy specialized in losing track of his sentences while showing off his huge vocabulary and not saying much of anything.

I made the mistake of checking to see if Jeff thought they looked as ridiculous as I did. Unfortunately, his adorable smile made my craving to hug him almost unbearable, and against my will, I started thinking of sentences like "I really miss you," and "Will you swear on your life that you will *never* reveal the truth if we just share one teeny, tiny kiss?"

In one last attempt to get control of my pounding heart, I thought of Cara. I pictured her looking at me in the hall near the boiler room, saying she thought everybody cheated. And I heard my own words assuring her that I certainly didn't. I saw her expression change as she decided to stay loyal to the cause. She did it out of faith in *you*! I shouted in my mind, as Jeff's shining green eyes turned to meet mine.

Could I possibly have had the strength to resist betraying my beliefs? If I surrendered my principles just long enough for one little kiss, could I have refused the next? These are questions I'll never know the answers to because, as though sent by fate either to rescue or torment me, Dunk and Wally burst through the door at just that moment.

"Is it over? Is it over?" Wally puffed, purple-faced.

"Sure is," Jeff replied disgustedly.

"I thought you were eating at Wally's," I said to Dunk.

Since he was still mad at me, he ignored me and looked right at Jeff when he answered my question. "Nah. Not after we found out Mrs. Peters was going to spring liver on us. We cut out fast. Did we really miss it? We ran all the way. Well, what's for dinner here?" he asked. No offer, of course, to help cook anything.

"Eggplant gunk," I answered. For the first time in years, I was actually glad to have Dunk interrupt me.

Chapter Nine

By the time I met Jeff the next day after practice, I had convinced myself that it was willpower rather than obnoxious-brother-power that kept me from kissing him. It seemed to me for the first time that we were actually winning Lizzie's War. Most of the girls were now wearing gold pins and, like me, bravely resisting temptation. The boys knew their team would have trouble winning a single game without girls to cheer them on. (Parsons was definitely the worst team in the league.) We girls even had a big rally planned for the middle of the next week. By the time the vote came up, the boys wouldn't dare go against us!

So I was really happy that Friday, and I stayed happy until Jeff told me his little surprise as we walked home. "Listen," he said, "we're taking our vote on Monday."

"What?" I knew in a flash that could spell disaster for us. The pressure was building fast, but I knew it hadn't yet cracked the leaders of the boys' team, Jim, Dunk and Gordy.

"The will *gives* us a month," Jeff explained, "but we don't have to *take* a month."

"That's not fair," I snapped. "You're so superior about respecting the dead guy's wishes and being so self-righteous, but you're perfectly happy to go along with a dirty little trick like this."

"I'm not just going along with it, I *invented* it. I set it up with Jim and the coach. As soon as my plan is ready, we're going to call a vote. And today I told the guys it'll be ready Monday."

So this was Jeff's secret weapon for ending Lizzie's War! "But why?" I asked.

"I don't think the girls' plan is right. Now we're going to take our vote, and it'll be over. No more Lizzie's War."

"And no more having our floor fixed. That's what you're really doing, ruining our only chance."

"I told you, I'd do everything I could. I've

worked hard on my plan, and I think it'll be a success."

"Plan?" I shouted angrily. "What plan? How come *I* never heard about any great plan?" I sounded as bad as Jeff had when I'd told him about Lizzie's War the first time.

"It was none of your business. I told you it was up to the boys, remember?"

"Oh, yeah," I growled, my hands clenched into two angry fists. "I remember every stupid thing you said, and you can go think up any plans you like as long as *I'm not in them!*"

Then I saw the hurt in those adorable green eyes. No, I didn't bite my tongue off and kick my shins and apologize for saying the dumbest thing in the world. I just ran home and flung myself sobbing on the bed. What else could I do?

If you think I've already described some uncomfortable moments at the Bennet dinner table, the worst is still to come. That night was the pits. Dunk had gotten word a few days earlier that the school wanted his Camaro out of the parking lot, so he'd had it towed and then parked it in front of the house. He was really worried that the sight of it would get Dad worked up at him. Dad was really upset by the pressure the senator's assistant had put on him. The fact that he and Dunk still hadn't made up from their last argument put him in an even worse mood. I knew Dad hadn't forgiven Dunk for what he'd said about the audit. And it wasn't like Dunk to apologize, either. The tension between Dad and Dunk had Mom keyed up and looking for some place to dump *her* tension. And my furious break-up with Jeff made me feel like one of those earthworms you see stranded on the sidewalk after a summer rainstorm.

I don't even remember what we had for dinner. Dad opened the conversation by saying he'd written Senator Fleming a letter saying he was quitting the state highway audit because he had better things to do than work for crooks. He didn't say it to anyone in particular, and we were all too depressed to comment.

Well, we were all sitting around picking at our food and not saying a word, when Dad's self-control sprang a leak. "How long are you going to leave that junkpile on the street?" he said, staring at Dunk.

"I don't know."

Mom and I caught the wobble in Dunk's voice, but I guess Dad didn't. "I want an answer," he said. All he got was a shrug. "Douglas, I've had a bellyful of you. And I'm not just talking about the car. I'm talking about your stubborn, childish attitude in this basketball issue at the school. I really would expect a son of mine—"

"Excuse me," I said loudly.

"What?" Dad certainly hadn't expected me to stick up for Dunk.

"That's between us," I said.

"Oh, *is* it, my pet?"

"Richard!"

"I'm dealing with the children."

Mom stood up, turned, and walked out of the room. It was the best thing to do under the circumstances. Then Dad stood up, too. He flung his napkin down and went after her. Dunk and I listened to both sets of feet hurrying up the stairs, and then came angry whispers.

If I'd had any appetite to start with, it certainly would have been demolished by then, but even empty, my stomach did this really weird flip-flop as soon as I looked up and saw Dunk's face. I have *never* seen my brother look so sad. I looked around the dining room about ninety-seven times, trying to think of something to say. Dunk beat me to it.

"I'm a toad," he said. "You know why I lost my car? Because I didn't have the brains to put oil in it. You know why I told Dad to go be a crook when he asked me about the audit? Because I was ashamed of myself for not doing anything when Gordy got on your case. Not even in the lockers after. I was ashamed of myself for not doing the right thing, so I tried to make it sound like there wasn't any good reason for Dad to do the right thing, either. It was like a way of pretending to myself that doing the right thing doesn't matter. Y'know?"

"Yeah, I think so."

He shook his head. "Wally's the closest friend I've got, and I messed him up so bad with Lizzie, she won't have anything to do with him."

"Yeah."

His eyes were pretty moist by now, and I really hoped he wouldn't cry. "You know what Dad thinks of me? He thinks I'm a moron lowlife toad with no morals."

"I don't know."

"You know what Kathy said to me this afternoon?"

I wished I were somewhere else. Anywhere. I'd never seen Dunk like this, and it was pretty depressing.

"What?"

"She told me I don't have normal feelings. She said I'm acting so much of the time I don't know what's going on inside me and she pities me. And it's over with us."

I tried to swallow, but I couldn't.

"What about Janie and Moira?"

He shrugged his shoulders feebly. Kathy had been the only one of his girlfriends he was really serious about. "All three of them finally got together," he whispered. "Kathy said they had a good laugh."

Well, that started me crying. I mean, he looked so pitiful. Dunk left a little while after that, put on his coat, and went out the front door.

I cleared the table, stored the untouched food in plastic containers, and did the dishes. Then I went up to my room, stuck a piece of paper with carbon and second sheet into the typewriter, put the date on the top, and wrote:

I Douglas Bennet, promise, swear, assure, and give my solemn word and oath to repay $900 to my sister, Marlene Lenore Bennet, out of my lifeguard pay in the following installments: $300 on the last day of June, July, and August. Also, I promise to pay whatever interest that money would have earned if it had been in the bank all along. This agreement becomes legal after I sign it, and the minute Marlene Lenore Bennet gives me the money mentioned above, namely $900.

Signed_____

Douglas Bennet

I spent the next two hours trying to study. Dunk got home about ten. By then Mom had stopped by my room two or three times to ask where he was.

I knew I'd have Dunk to myself for a few minutes at least, because he came up the stairs barefoot, and when he does that, I'm the only one who can hear him. I guess he didn't want to get into a hassle with Mom and Dad about going out and worrying them for hours.

"Where'd you go?" I asked, poking my head into his room. He didn't look any happier than when he'd left.

"Archie's," he said and sighed.

I handed him the paper. His forehead wrinkled as he read. "How come you're lending me your money?" he asked.

"I need the rides home after practice."

"Yeah? You've been doing fine without them so far."

Then he said, "I know why." Tears started forming in his big brown eyes.

"Why?" I croaked.

"Because you pity me."

"No!" I got it out pretty forcefully, which made him forget about crying. "I stabbed you in the back worse than you ever did to me. Believe me, I'm a worse lowlife than you are. I'm just apologizing for that." He looked at me like I'd stepped off the plane from Saturn. "I told Moira your nightmare story was a phony and that you used it on two other girls. I heard you bragging to Wally, and I told her in Lizzie's basement during the big meeting."

He didn't say anything else, so after a little while, I left. Dunk was sitting on the edge of his bed with the piece of paper next to him and the picture of Gloria Glory grinning down at him.

Chapter Ten

"Read this." Jeff's voice was not warm, but you could have considered it almost friendly if you made the effort, which I did. He'd caught up to me about a block from school Monday morning and shoved a sheet of paper at me.

It didn't take long to read. Under the heading, "Plan for Spending Basketball Money," Jeff had typed the following:

    New Scoreboard: $2500
    Ten Uniforms, Boys' Team: $900
    Repairs to Girls' Practice Foor: $1600
    Repaint Bleachers: No Charge

"Well written," I said, trying to digest it quickly.

"It took my father all week to line up the bid for the floor work. He had to make about three dozen calls around the state before finding people in his business who would do the school a favor and work really cheaply. The other floor repair prices were at least twice that much."

"How are you going to get the bleachers painted for free?" I asked.

"The paint isn't much if you get it wholesale, so my father said he'd contribute that for good will in the neighborhood."

"But who's going to paint them?"

"Us. Both teams. We can paint them in a day, easy."

Suddenly, I felt my temper jump. "You are going to drive me completely crazy, Jeff Simmons."

"What do you mean?" Jeff asked, confused. "I thought you'd be wild over getting the new floor."

"It's just that if we had more time, I bet we could actually get your moron friends to *vote* for your plan."

I could see that upset him. "You want to argue or something? I did the best I could."

"All right, I'm sorry," I said. "But what if you lose the vote this afternoon?"

"There's nothing I can do about it. Are you going to hold a grudge?"

I shrugged. He took my hand. You will recall that hand holding was a major no-no at the time? Well, I would certainly have stopped him except that he looked right into my eyes when he did it.

As we walked into school, though, I did wonder how I'd feel about him if he lost. Why did he have to be so *sure* of himself? Why did he have to do it his *own* stupid way? Why couldn't he just have stuck with Lizzie and me? Still, I was in total bliss to be with him.

At least until we started getting comments in the hall. The first was "Traitor." I didn't even know the girl who said it. But she probably thought I'd been sneaking around with Jeff all week.

Then Julia spotted us. "Oh, Marley," she said, then sighed. There was no anger in her voice, only disappointment. Well, let me tell you, there was nothing I wanted more than to drop Jeff's hand, but I just couldn't do it. I couldn't hurt him after he'd done his best for the girls.

Then, as if he were reading my mind, he let go of my hand and said, "I have to make a confession to you."

My knees got a little rubbery. A million

horrible thoughts whizzed through my brain. Someone else *had* moved in after all our recent arguments. Or he'd started his North Carolina romance up again long distance and was going there to spend the summer with his grandparents. Or the flame had just gone out of our relationship without any fuel to keep it going.

He tilted his head a little. "This is kind of hard for me to say."

"Yeah? Well?"

"I haven't been entirely honest with you."

"Oh?" I forced myself to sound casual.

"You know how I've been talking about respecting the dead guy's will and all?" I nodded. "And how it's wrong for the girls to be taking matters into their own hands for that reason?" Another nod. "Well, I really believe all that. But it's not the main reason I wanted to stop Lizzie's War."

"No?" Now I was totally confused.

"No. It was you."

"What?"

He smiled a little. "I want us to be together. Do you understand?" I gulped. It was the best I could do. "And I knew you wouldn't change your mind, even if you really wanted to. I knew you would hold out as long as the war lasted."

"You think so?" I said. He sounded a lot more sure than I ever was. But he seemed to know what he was talking about.

"Yes," he replied.

"Maybe. Maybe I would've—"

"Given in?" he finished my sentence for me. "Like on Thursday night? Well, if you did, you'd be really mad at yourself. And sooner or later I'd catch some of the blame. But this way, it's just over. I stopped Lizzie's War because I thought it was wrong. But I did it mainly because I can't stop thinking about you."

He bent down to kiss me, right there in the hallway. But luckily for me—the girls would never have talked to me again if he had—two of Jeff's friends came along, slapped his back, and practically dragged him down the hall.

So there I was, alone in the hallway with some pretty difficult questions. For example, since Jeff ended Lizzie's War mainly so I wouldn't have to stay away from him, *did that mean it was my fault?* And how would I feel about him when the boys voted down his plan? Would I ever be able to forgive him for ruining our chances of getting a new floor? Would I just rush into his arms and forget everything? Now, more than ever, I felt completely and utterly miserable.

The rest of the day dragged along. You know how when you're waiting for something the minutes just creep by? That's how I felt. I didn't even have a chance to talk to any of the other girls. I spotted Lizzie in the hall between classes, and she gave me the thumbs-up sign. I figured she was just being cheerful in the face of disaster. I was sure Jeff's plan would lose.

Anyway, one long class followed another, but finally the last bell rang, and I tromped over to the annex gym for practice, after which we'd find out the results of the boys' vote. All of a sudden, it seemed like the event I'd been waiting for all day had come too soon. In about an hour, we'd know for sure that we were doomed to slip and stick and hurt ourselves forever on that rotten floor.

"Oh, girls?" Ms. Bullfinch's English accent sounded slightly muffled through the locker room door. "May I come in for a moment?" We were all in the locker room after practice, hurrying to change so we could wait in the hall for the guys to come out of the gym with their verdict. "I have some jolly splendid news for you."

We looked at each other. Big grins passed from face to face. Everyone started shouting and jumping around. "C'mon in, C'mon in!"

Only as the door inched open did I guess the truth. It was my rotten brother Dunk doing another one of his amazing imitations. Of course, the sight of his extremely evil grin caused all kinds of shrieks. After the first sneaker whizzed by his head, every girl in the room let something fly at him. Still, we were so desperate for the truth that Lizzie tore out of the locker room in her sweat clothes to drag Dunk back. By the time she did, we were all dressed.

Dunk just said, "The vote was almost unanimous. Your floor gets fixed over Christmas vacation." Well, we were all too stunned at the incredibly fantastic news to ask questions, and that's how Dunk escaped without giving us any details about what had happened. I had to wait for my walk home with Jeff to hear them.

It was a beautiful sunny day, so Jeff and I took the long route home. The first thing I did was apologize to him for not believing his plan would work and for being so moody with him. Then he apologized to me for not letting me in on his idea for solving the basketball money problem earlier. Then we kissed and hugged for the first time in one long, difficult week. That was the best part. After that, I got the full story on the vote.

At first, the boys were about equally split between Jeff and Jim's plans.

Gordy Fellows got up and said some witty, nasty things about Lizzie, and he said basically that he hated being pushed and that it was the guys' turn to push back. He said he was voting for Jim's plan, and a lot of the boys agreed.

Then Dunk got up and—surprise of surprises—said, "The girls are right. Their floor's no good. I wouldn't play on it. I've got a sister always coming home with some story about how someone slipped and hurt herself. If it came down to us giving up what we want for them, it would be different. But it doesn't. It's no good sticking them with a lousy floor while we blow the money on stuff nobody needs. I'm voting for Jeff's plan. And I'm glad he got us all off the hook by giving us a way to do the right thing and still get the equipment we need."

Jeff said that Dunk's speech was a real shock to the boys. But not compared to what happened next. Jim got up and said he didn't want his girlfriend slipping and hurting herself. Which was strange because Jim didn't go out with anyone on the girls' team. Yet. But whatever his motive, he actually did an about-face and spoke out against his own plan. With Dunk and Jim, two of the ring-leaders, voting for Jeff's plan, the rest of the team followed along pretty quickly. Gordy ended up being the only one to vote against us.

Jeff told the story so well that I just *had* to kiss him all over again. Then we walked the rest of the way home, and Mom invited him to stay for dinner after I told her about how he'd gotten us our floor. You can't imagine how happy we all were.

But that was nothing compared to my dad when he got home from work a little later. He threw me a kiss from across the living room, then dashed into the kitchen where my mom was making dinner. I heard Mom give a shriek, which sounded a whole lot like one of Dunk's Kung Fu victory cries, and Jeff and I ran in to see what was going on.

"I got a call from Senator Fleming," Dad explained, smiling like mad. "I've still got the audit, and the Senator's *former* assistant is under investigation for trying to interfere with my work!"

"Yippee," I cried, "I guess honesty really is the best policy."

"You bet!" Dad said.

"Great, then I'll tell you straight out. I told Dunk last night that he can borrow all the money I've saved up for a new motor for his car."

"What about your summer trip?" Dad asked.

"It's just not that important to me. Dunk needs his car more than I need the trip."

"That's very generous of you," Dad said.

"Excellent," Jeff whispered. We walked into the living room, and he said softly in my ear, "I'm glad you're not going to Pike's Peak. I always hoped we'd spend the summer together."

"But the tour was only three weeks."

Jeff smiled. "I always thought that was *much* too long." Then I felt his arms around me once again, and I had to admit, three weeks away from him would feel like ages.

Epilogue

It's early August right now. So far, Dunk's made his payments right on time. What's more, we got Jeff to teach us both about fixing up cars. Dunk spends a lot of time working on the Camaro, and Jeff says that with all we've put into it, it's a really fine old machine. Dad's incredibly impressed, and he's always asking Dunk to check this and that on the station wagon.

It also seems Kathy didn't get such a big laugh swapping tales about Dunk with Moira and Janie. In fact, she and Dunk patched it up, and are getting along better than ever. Dunk doesn't see other girls, and he's more open and honest with Kathy. I wish I could say the same thing for Lizzie and Wally. Unfortunately, the trials of the basketball battle were too much for them, and they don't see each other any more.

And what about Jim's mysterious girlfriend on the team? Remember when Cara wanted to go on a date with him? Well, they've been going out ever since Lizzie's War was called off.

Our new floor is a dream, and the main gym looks great, too. We all had a fantastic time painting the bleachers. When I come back to visit good old Riverport High after I graduate, I'll always be able to find the place where I swirled my initials into the paint. Now the bleachers are sort of a monument to us all.

Dad's audit went beautifully, and Bennet Accounting has two new accountants, a new computer, and a bigger office. I'm helping out there for the summer and learning some really great stuff about the computer. After work I usually meet Jeff, who's helping his father build houses this summer. Sometimes we go over to the park and shoot baskets. And sometimes we don't.

Don't miss any of these great new *Sweet Dreams* romances, on sale soon!

☐ **#61 EXCHANGE OF HEARTS by Janet Quin-Harkin (On sale April 15, 1984 • 24056-0 • $2.25)**
Fiona's not enjoying her stay as an exchange student in New Mexico: she misses her boyfriend Simon back in England, and Taco West, the only boy on the ranch she's staying at, teases her and treats her like a pesky kid sister. But as time goes by, Fiona finds that Taco has a tender side too. Should she stay faithful to the boy she's supposed to love— or give her heart to the boy she thought she hated?

☐ **#62 JUST LIKE THE MOVIES by Suzanne Rand (On sale April 15, 1984 • 24057-9 • $2.25)**
Marcy wants to be an actress. So when she gets a walk-on part in teen idol Lance Newmark's new movie, she puts all her time and energy into getting more scenes—and more attention from Lance. Her old friends are quickly becoming strangers, but it will be worth it when she's a star and has the boy she's always dreamed about. Won't it?

☐ **THE SWEET DREAMS MAKEUP WORKBOOK: A GUIDE TO GLOWING SKIN AND A PRETTIER YOU by Patricia Bozic (On sale April 15, 1984 • 24165-6 • $2.25)**
Beauty's only skin deep . . . but your skin *is* one of the first things people notice about you. If you want to put your best face forward, start with THE SWEET DREAMS MAKEUP

WORKBOOK. It's a surefire guide to glowing skin and professional-looking makeup, containing tips on fragrances, lips, lashes, superclean skin, and everything else you need to make the most of your natural beauty.

☐ **#63 KISS ME, CREEP by Marian Woodruff (On sale May 15, 1984 • 24150-8 • $2.25)**
Every girl at Cabrillo High has a crush on Richie Brennan—except Joy Wilder. She can't stand his smug, conceited attitude or his stupid jokes, especially the romantic ones: he always kids Joy about being in love with her. Then one day she discovers that he's more serious than she thought. Is Richie really a creep—or someone Joy can love?

☐ **#64 LOVE IN THE FAST LANE by Rosemary Vernon (On sale May 15, 1984 • 24151-6 • $2.25)**
When Alison's boyfriend died in a car race, she didn't think she could ever get over him—until the day she met Billy Kendall. But soon Alison discovers Billy's enthusiasm for motocross, and it seems as if she's doomed to lose the boy she loves . . . again.

Buy these books at your local bookstore or use this handy coupon for ordering:

*Share the continuing story of
the Wakefield twins and their friends at*

SWEET VALLEY
HIGH

Created by Francine Pascal

Come to Sweet Valley High and get swept up in all
the romance, drama, thrills, and heartbreak of
high school life. Enter its halls and meet identical
twins Elizabeth and Jessica Wakefield. Elizabeth
is the caring school journalist who is everybody's
friend. Jessica is the beautiful, coquettish captain
of the cheering squad—and the most conniving
sixteen-year-old ever to strut down a school corridor.
Look for this exciting new series of novels wherever
Bantam paperbacks are sold—there's a new one on
sale every month!

☐ **#5 ALL NIGHT LONG (On sale January 15,
1984 • 23943-0 • $2.25)**
Jessica's forbidden overnight partying leaves Liz
to play the toughest dramatic role of her life. It's
one thing to be a stand-in for her twin at the
breakfast table, but to take a crucial test for her is
another matter. . . .

☐ **#6 DANGEROUS LOVE (On sale February 15,
1984 • 23938-4 • $2.25)**
One of the only hard-and-fast rules in the Wakefield
household is no motorcycles. So imagine Liz's
surprise when a beaming Todd shows up with a
huge new Yamaha for which he's scrimped and
saved—not to mention sold his car.

☐ #7 DEAR SISTER (On sale March 15, 1984 • 24001-3 • $2.25)

Liz has completely recovered from her motorcycle accident—or has she? Lately she's been acting more like Jessica than her normal self. Her grades are slipping, she's in trouble with the school paper—and she's suddenly a lot more interested in Bruce Patman than Todd Wilkins.

☐ #8 HEARTBREAKER (On sale April 15, 1984 • 24045-5 • $2.25)

Jessica's been cast as the lead in the school play, along with handsome surfer Bill Chase—who's very interested in doing some extracurricular scenes with her. Meanwhile, Todd's old girlfriend Patsy has shown up in town, and he doesn't have quite as much time for Elizabeth. . . .

☐ #9 LOVE ON THE RUN (On sale May 15, 1984 • 24131-1 • $2.25)

Roger Barrett, the poorest boy in Sweet Valley, enters a running race to win a scholarship to Sweet Valley College. But his secret employment as a janitor prevents him from practicing for the competition—and from getting together with rich girl Lila Fowler, who has been paying lots of attention to him now that he may be the next school star.

Buy these books at your local bookstore or use this handy coupon for ordering:

SPECIAL
MONEY SAVING
OFFER

Now you can have an up-to-date listing of Bantam's hundreds of titles plus take advantage of our unique and exciting bonus book offer. A special offer which gives you the opportunity to purchase a Bantam book for only 50¢. Here's how!

By ordering any five books at the regular price per order, you can also choose any other single book listed (up to a $4.95 value) for just 50¢. Some restrictions do apply, but for further details why not send for Bantam's listing of titles today!

Just send us your name and address plus 50¢ to defray the postage and handling costs.